# THE DEMON'S EYE

## JON DEL ARROZ

RISLANDIA BOOKS

# NEWSLETTER

Want to keep up to date on news, new releases, and convention appearances? Join the JDA Newsletter!

1

HOOVES SLOSHED IN THE MIDDLE OF THE MUDDY STREETS OF ANTIOCH, spraying a puddle of sludge on a couple walking. The citizens of Tyril's largest city gasped at getting doused, but they had little recourse for their indignity. Recent rains turned all of Antioch into a mess akin to the worst war-torn towns in the Sorcerer King's aggressions. But even with mud-splattered buildings and the grime covering the common folks' boots, the air had a fresh smell compared to the hot, summer season which had a putrid stench much like rotting meat.

Jayden leaned against a local tavern with his gittern in hand, case laid open at his feet, trying to get the attention of drunken passersby to give him coin.

It hadn't been a poor start to the night, with at least twenty coppers thrown into his case, but coppers wouldn't last him long after lodging and food.

He strummed his gittern and sang a tune of ancient battles gone by. His voice was deep and pleasant, at least so many fair ladies had told him. Even with a good voice, he had to be careful singing the songs ingrained in his memory, as most ballads he'd learned featured

Hyrum warriors as heroes. The Tyril people did not look kindly upon their neighboring kingdom.

It had been five long years since the war ravaged these lands, but hostilities were still as strong as ever. Some Tyril people scowled at him because of the angular nature of his face and his bright green eyes, a highlight of Hyrum lineage. But most of these folk had probably never encountered a Hyrum warrior in their lives—at least, they wouldn't realize they had.

His voice carried well, despite the cold. An hour of singing already had warmed his vocal cords and given a nice, raspy quality to his voice. He belted about heroes long past, a tune old enough that either the Tyril people wouldn't remember, or they wouldn't be offended by the praising of Hyrum warriors. It was a song of kings and betrayals, loves and losses, battles and brothers. Jayden put all the passion he could muster into the songs, even as a group of drunken men stumbled out of the tavern.

Three of them approached, one barely able to walk. The other two held him upright so he wouldn't fall face-first into the muddy street.

"Careful, Garid," one said.

"I can walk by myself, Mergin," Garid said, flailing his arms to get his friends off of him. As he did, his head bobbled to a position where his eyes rested firmly on Jayden. Those brown, Tyril-born eyes narrowed on him.

Jayden sang through the distraction, having faced far worse in his time as a bard. While busking on the street, he often found himself faced with drunks, or carriages making loud noises, or sometimes even teenagers hounding him. After five years of the meager work, he was prepared for almost anything the streets could throw at him.

Almost.

"Dirty, bloody Hyrum," Garid muttered, stumbling forward. His momentum carried him all the way over, causing him to crash into Jayden.

Jayden braced himself against the wall but couldn't keep strumming his gittern while being tackled. The drunk had ruined the song. There was little he could do to recover. The shock of the man's full-body impact into his torso caused him to expend his air. The last note he sang turned into a much higher, shriller sound than he had intended.

Garid's friends laughed, while the drunken man tried to regain his footing.

"M'lord, I hope you're okay. If you enjoyed the music s'much, could you spare a c—"

Garid answered Jayden by throwing a fist to his face.

Not expecting violence, Jayden absorbed the blow. The man's fist hit him high on the cheekbone, impacting with loose knuckles rather than a tight fist—this was no trained warrior. Regardless of the man's fighting capabilities, however, the hit stung.

Jayden reacted the way he'd been trained, instinctual self-defense taking over his every movement. He shoved his gittern toward Garid, forcing the man back, and also making him lose his balance. Garid fell on his ass, mud splattering where he hit the ground.

"Dirty Hyrum thinks he can fight us," Mergin said.

"Let's show him what for," said their third companion.

This wasn't good. While he could easily fend off one drunk, even if these weren't men trained to fight, the numbers were against him.

He didn't carry a weapon. With his Hyrum features, he wanted to appear as harmless as possible, which had worked so far. He didn't want any trouble with the local magistrates.

Trouble looked unavoidable.

The two other Tyril helped Garid to his feet, and Jayden backed away from the scene. Garid kicked over Jayden's gittern case, coppers flying out into the street, covered in mud. Some would be impossible to find, even if he won this fight.

His entire night's work would be for naught. Jayden's stomach grumbled as he considered the food he wouldn't be able to purchase.

He backpedaled before making a turn so he could run faster. The three men gave pursuit, their boots sloshing in the mud with each step. From the sounds of it, they were close.

Jayden clutched his gittern, running as hard as he could, until he reached an area in a back alley where the walls closed in on him. He'd turned into a dead end. He was trapped.

Turning, he came face to face with the three men who chased him. Blood rage filled their eyes. They hated him for being Hyrum, they hated what he represented to them. Nothing he could say would sway them. From the looks of the streets, there would be no one to cry out to, either. Shadows fell over everything, the night unbearably dark.

Mergin attacked him first, driving a blow into Jayden's torso. The attack hit the gittern instead, the Tyril's fist impaling the instrument.

The gittern cracked. Strings broke. The instrument of his livelihood destroyed.

Anger flared in Jayden, a heat he needed to keep tempered within him. The emotional wounds of battle were still fresh, even five years later, and he wanted to keep them at bay.

These men had not afforded him the chance.

He lifted his broken gittern and bashed Mergin across the head with it. The man went down, and the gittern broke in two. He had a small stick now, but it was more than the other men had.

With alcohol flowing through their veins, however, they couldn't make reasonable judgments. Both remaining Tyril rushed him. Garid slammed Jayden against the wall, and the third man grabbed him by the arm so he couldn't use the neck of his gittern as a bludgeon.

As much as he had the edge from sobriety and from his former training as a warrior, their numbers proved overwhelming as he had feared. Jayden kneed Garid in the stomach, but the man was already too far gone to feel pain.

Garid swung wildly, connecting a lucky blow to Jayden's temple. The world went fuzzy with the hard hit. As he came to from spinning, Jayden found he had lost his footing and fell to the ground.

The two men kicked him repeatedly. There was little Jayden could do but try to block the blows with his elbows, and even then, several of the hard kicks got through, striking his legs, his ribs, his head. What had he done to deserve such a fate? All he had been trying to do was make a career as a bard—a poor one at that—and this is how he had to go?

As the pain flared in his side, he expected the world to go dark, but instead, he saw a bright light coming straight for him like an arrow flung from a bow.

* * *

THE LIGHT WASHED OVER JAYDEN, gentle, like foam from the waves of the ocean crashing against the shore. It was so bright, however, he could hardly see the figure standing in front of him.

The creature was whiter than white, a pure lack of color he could hardly describe. It looked vaguely human—a woman? It was hard to say. Flowing robes fell over the creature's body, and long hair draped over its chest. In its hands was a golden harp.

It played a tune, a song in a major key, uplifting and airy, much like the harpist itself. The tune sounded classic, ancient even. The song resonated through Jayden's soul, calling to him like the creature had written it for him specifically. What could it mean?

Jayden tried to crawl backward, but he found himself unable to move. What was this place? What was going on?

His chest tightened, and he panicked. What if he were dead? This could be some creature luring him into the afterlife.

The creature played its song without caring for Jayden's reactions. Once it finished, it let its hands drop, and it peered at Jayden.

He could see no eyes on the creature. Its face was fuzzy, non-distinct.

"Do not be afraid," the creature said. "But remember the song. The harp of ancients will end the tribulation."

"What's that supposed to mean?" Jayden asked, but before he could receive an answer, his world faded from view.

* * *

JAYDEN AWOKE to the sounds of something cracking and a person crying out in pain. He stirred where he lay crumpled in the alley, alert and sensing danger about his person.

Everything hurt. His ribs, his face, his body in terrible shape, probably worse than the gittern he'd used as a bludgeon against his attackers.

How long had it been? There was no way to tell, but it was still dark in the alley. Could his attackers still be nearby? Jayden glanced around.

Garid lay passed out in the alleyway, and the other two stumbled and grumbled in pain. A dark figure punched, kicked, slammed each of them against the wall. He handled both at once. He moved in a fluid manner, much quicker than the brute force Jayden used.

After the attackers took some punishment, they stumbled back from him. Then, the figure let a blade drop from each sleeve into his hands. Everything appeared as mere shadows in the darkness of the alley.

"You'll leave this fellow alone," the man said in a gruff voice.

"Let's get out of here," Mergin said.

"What about Garid?" the other man asked.

"He'll wake up later."

The two of them bolted down the alley and out of view.

The shadowy figure stood still for a while, but the other two didn't come back. Then he moved to Garid, who hadn't moved during this entire interchange. The figure pulled back his hood—a man with long, dark hair, and a beard to match. He frowned at Garid, rolling him over with the tip of his toe. "He'll not wake soon," he said.

"Savrin," Jayden said, recognizing the scruffy hair and chiseled facial structure. They'd met before, both men proclaimed as exiled from Hyrum. Jayden helped Savrin cross the border into Umdarsh, which may have well saved his life from the wrath of the Sorcerer King. "What are you doing in Antioch?"

"I would ask you much the same," Savrin said, offering a hand to Jayden, "but it appears the answer is causing trouble. Were you singing songs about the ancient Hyrum knight orders again? I told you it would upset people in Tyril."

Jayden grunted but took the man's hand and the assistance to his feet. The world still swam about in swirls, pain flaring and dimming with each breath. He found it difficult to stand, and his ribs hurt from being kicked.

"It's divine providence that I come across you here," Savrin said. "I'm in need of a sturdy blade for a quest I've accepted from Lord Hardwin."

"I've retired my blade, you know that," Jayden said, surveying the alley. His gittern would not be repairable. Another expense he'd have to incur when he found someone who crafted instruments. More coin he had to spend. Coin he didn't have. The thought made him frown.

"Ah, yes. For a new passion in music, was it?" Savrin's eyes flicked to Jayden's destroyed gittern and back. He gave a wry smirk. "Is your career going well for you?"

Jayden clenched his fist, fighting back an urge to sock the smirk off Savrin's face.

"Oh," Savrin said. "I'm sorry. Well, will you at least hear me out?"

"We should get out of here before the local magistrates find some of their own bloodied on the street by two Hyrum," Jayden said. He stepped over the body and made his way out of the alley.

Savrin jogged to catch up. The streets were emptier than before, with a darkened night sky. It would have been a bad evening for busking, anyway. "I have a little room in the inn down the way. You're welcome to join me."

Jayden said nothing. He would have been sleeping on the streets tonight, as he did most evenings when he played in a city like this. During the best of times, he found work on farms, helping with manual labor during the day, and he would often receive lodging for it. Those jobs had dried up in recent weeks, with the harvest having passed. Savrin didn't need to know this, however. He could retain some of his dignity. "Lead the way."

They walked along until they came to the inn, and Savrin opened the main door to allow them inside. Their common room had very little going on, unlike the tavern where Jayden had been singing.

Savrin helped himself to the bar, where there was no attendant currently.

"Are you sure we shouldn't ask for someone?"

"I know the owner," Savrin said.

He poured two glasses of wine and set them down at a table. "Please," he said.

Jayden sat and took one of the wine glasses. He drank. It had been awhile since he could afford wine, and though this was not the best quality, the sweetness was a welcome taste to his tongue.

Savrin dropped back the whole glass in one gulp. "Ahh," he said afterward, setting it down.

"You're uncivilized," Jayden said.

"Being in the muck of battle for some king who means nothing to you will do that," Savrin said.

"And serving Lord Hardwin?" Jayden raised a brow.

"Lord Hardwin pays handsomely. Which I believe you could use to your advantage, could you not?" Savrin grinned.

"Depends. I don't want to do violence."

"Violence may or may not come. What I'm talking about is adventuring."

"Have you had too much to drink already?"

Savrin slapped his hands on the table. "I'm just getting started. And when we're done, we might be able to afford some of the best wine from the Freelands."

"But you say we're working for Lord Hardwin. won't he take a cut?"

Savrin leaned in. "Hardwin has discovered a map, one which outlines the ancients' holds from the first days. It's got treasures, and he wants us to go get them."

"Us?"

"Well, me. I'm hiring you on retainer."

"I didn't agree to this yet. You didn't tell me where we're going, how long will this be, how we'll get *food* along the way." Jayden took another sip of the wine. Perhaps his friend had the right of it with the way he downed his drink.

Savrin scratched his head. "Hardwin will cover it."

"He will? What's the catch?"

"No catch!"

Jayden shook his head. "This sounds too good to be true. Either there's going to be an extreme amount of danger, or there's something else going on I can't quite put my finger on."

"Ranger's oath, I promise it's true." Savrin held up three fingers.

Jayden glowered at him. "You're not a ranger."

"True, but regardless, this is the best thing you have going for you. I promise, our food is covered. We're going to do some exploring. It'll be fun. And if there's a magnificent prize at the end of it, so much the better, eh?" His grin returned.

Jayden sighed. It wasn't as if he had much choice. He didn't have many prospects for the winter for work, and he couldn't play any longer. At least not until he could afford a new instrument. "Fine. When do we leave?"

* * *

After a week of sailing, Jayden found himself in the Freelands. The cold bit through to his bones. He couldn't imagine living this far north, but no one complained about the air they could see when they exhaled. It wasn't even the dead of winter yet. In another month or two, it would be even worse.

Sailors bustled around the port, with several ships offloading supplies, adding more cargo of various animal pelts from the region. The Freelands exported the finest furs, though he'd never been able to afford one. Here, though, Jayden could purchase a fur-lined coat for next to nothing. Transport and duties escalated costs beyond comprehension. Savrin got them both new coats the moment they got off the dock, for which Jayden was grateful—but he grumbled about being beholden to his friend.

This whole quest still resonated wrong with him. It wouldn't turn out as simple as Savrin made it sound. He could feel it in his bones as much as the chill in the air. He'd retired from the hard life, or so he'd thought. Not that attempting to be a bard had been much easier than being a soldier or sellsword. In many ways, he struggled more than ever before. As an army man, he never had to worry where his next meal came from. Still, if this Lord Hardwin could pay as well as Savrin implied, Jayden had little other choice.

But could he trust his former colleague? No matter how Jayden tried, Savrin wouldn't talk about how he got so close with this Lord Hardwin, or what the lord hoped to accomplish through their efforts beyond mere treasure. Something smelled fishy, and Savrin had fallen for schemes in the past. They'd separated before because Savrin attempted to join some band of unscrupulous mercenaries, while Jayden wanted nothing more to do with fighting. Savrin nearly lost a limb, but in some ways he'd come out ahead of Jayden. At least the efforts had brought him to this lord patron who provided for them.

"We'll find a place to sleep and head out in the morning," Savrin said, giving Jayden a slap to the back.

Jayden let out a deep breath as they walked into town. Beyond, the Mount of Ancients peeked through the clouds. Snow covered the giant mountain, and they would have to traverse its rough terrain. He didn't look forward to it.

* * *

JAYDEN AND SAVRIN met with a local guide named Luice. Savrin offered a couple of coppers, and the guide was happy to show him the path to the The Mount of the Ancients, though he shook his head and muttered about them being fools. They rose at dawn, packs full with food, water, and extra layers of clothing to shield them from the elements. Flakes of snow fluttered even to the lower elevations of the town, near the sea, but melted as soon as they hit the ground.

Walking along in the cold proved difficult on the muscles, bringing Jayden back to memories of being in Hyrum's infantry regiment, hiking for days before hitting the next enemy target. He'd endured worse, and with far fewer provisions than he had now. As it stood, they'd left the inn on a full stomach after drinking hot tea to keep them warm. For a time, Jayden even sweated as they hiked.

Why had he agreed to go with Savrin? The discomfort alone hardly made this worth it, and he could tell from the look of the clouds up at higher elevations their path would become far more perilous. He wouldn't have had better prospects back home. He had already burned too many bridges with his own people and the neighboring nation. Every night he played in some inn was merely another night someone might drive a dagger into his back. Die there or die here, he supposed.

The cold became worse.

The sun never burned through the clouds. Instead, a blizzard formed. It appeared as a general snowstorm at first, and Luice didn't appear worried, but once they had hiked for most of the day, the winds picked up, the sky darkened, and the snow dropped in bigger clusters. The weather grew fierce.

A shriek sounded from a chasm up ahead. The men paused.

"Is that a dragon?" Savrin asked.

"There's no such thing as dragons," Jayden said, more to assuage his own fears and convince himself it was the case. Who knew what kind of foul creatures roamed the Freelands? "Probably just an animal caught out in this mess, scared for its life."

Luice shrugged, and the three men continued on.

"There will be small caves, maybe two hours walk from here," Luice said. "There, we can take shelter for the evening until the weather lets up."

They traversed along a wide chasm until they came to a rope bridge, frozen over in the elements. Luice tugged at the ropes, and they held. He stepped carefully onto the first rope and made his way across.

Ice slipped off of the rope, falling into a gorge below. The wind whistled, swaying them side to side as they tried to cross. It sent a chill up Jayden's spine.

Savrin lost his footing halfway across the gorge, but he gripped onto the rope with his hands, flailing off-balance. The idiot was always getting himself into trouble. Jayden peeled a hand from the ropes and helped Savrin regain his footing.

"Careful," Jayden said, trying to sound calmer than he truly felt of the matter. If he lost Savrin up here, what would he do?

"If anything was gonna wake me up and snap me to attention in this freezing cold, that was it," Savrin said, making light of what could have been his doom. The rogue took little seriously, and it made Jayden want to smack him upside the head to knock some sense into him.

They slowed their pace from that point and then stepped onto solid ground on the other side of the chasm.

Jayden regretted coming. He'd had misgivings and grumbled about the quest, but with the weather worsening and snow piling on so thick they couldn't see, he couldn't picture a happy ending to the journey.

Something screamed again. This time, the sound came from much closer than before.

Jayden turned, trying to see anything through the snow dumping across his vision. Endless white blinded him. How the guide even knew where to lead, he couldn't say. Keeping the guide within his line of sight proved difficult enough. But Luice continued on, and Jayden dutifully followed. They were too deep into the mountains for him to turn back now, alone. He would never find his way back to town.

They kept walking for what seemed an eternity before Savrin stopped in his tracks. "There's a woman up ahead," he said.

"I can't see anything," Jayden said.

"She's stuck in the snow... I have to help her." Savrin took off running ahead.

"Wait!" Luice said, but with the whistling wind, Savrin had already moved out of earshot.

He soon disappeared from sight.

"Fool," Jayden said to himself, trudging forward. Savrin had already nearly fallen to his doom, and now he rushed on ahead? The brazen rogue would be the death of all of them. Luice kept near to Jayden. It could take forever to find Savrin.

The weather proved to be a terrible obstacle, slowing their movements to a near standstill. The cold bit through to his bones far worse than before. The wind and sleet escalated. He had to shield his eyes.

When he found Savrin, the man lay on the ground, in a fetal position, shivering.

"What is bloody wrong with you?" Jayden asked.

He received his answer from a loud shriek directly in front of him.

A woman stood in the elements, but she floated in the air. Everything about her was as white as the snow—from her face, to her dress, to her hair, which stood up on its ends. She had a translucent quality to her. Jayden could see completely through her.

The woman rushed him, and the essence of her crossed through him.

Jayden gasped. At first, he couldn't breathe. His entire body froze over. He couldn't move. His muscles and joints locked. What devilry created this creature?

As soon as she passed through him, the cold subsided. This creature had something to do with the severity of the weather. The elements swirled around her like the eye of a storm.

Jayden turned around to geta better view, but the strange woman floated into their guide.

Savrin scrambled to his feet, seeming to have recovered. Much like Jayden, all he could do was stare as the blizzard woman writhed inside Luice, not passing through as she had done with Savrin and Jayden.

Luice convulsed. His mouth foamed, and his eyes rolled back in his head. He turned a pale blue, like the snow and ice from around them consumed him. This woman must be a demon—or perhaps something worse.

"My God," Savrin said. He fumbled inside of his thick fur coat.

"Why are we standing here? We need to get away from this demon before it consumes us as well," Jayden said.

"No. We'll never get away in time. I have a solution."

"Like when you ran after this spirit?" Jayden asked.

Savrin ignored him, stepping toward the convulsing Luice, who still had his eyes rolled up into his head, possessed. Their guide had also nearly frozen over. He hardly seemed human anymore—his body was almost as translucent as the woman's, an ice sculpture of himself.

His legs, which had turned into icicles, snapped at the convulsions. His torso slid off of his legs, onto the ground.

"Begone, spirit!" Savrin said. In his hand, he held a small gold chain with something dangling from it—difficult to make out in the blizzard.

The woman-spirit shrieked.

Savrin jabbed the chain closer to Luice's face.

The guide's head started spinning atop his neck in an intense circle, like travelers had said of the tornados above Demon's Eye Lake. The sight made Jayden's breath still. None of this could be real. This was insanity.

The wind and sleet formed such a funnel it became impossible to see. Jayden had to shield his eyes to keep snow from getting in them. The cold bit his clothing to his skin, causing him to shiver.

Then, as much as the weather had built to a dangerous whirlwind, it all stopped.

No more snow fell. No wind blew. The Mount of the Ancients fell into a peaceful silence. The sun peered through soft clouds, shining rays of light bringing warmth.

Jayden opened his eyes.

Luice collapsed backward falling face-first in the snow. His body had frozen over.

Savrin clutched his chain, holding his arm outstretched, eyes pressed tightly closed. The chain glimmered in the sun's soft rays, a small cross dangling from the end. A sign of the ancients' God, and one many to believed in to this day—especially those who dwelt in the Holy City.

"What are you doing?" Jayden asked.

Savrin opened his eyes, relaxed his shoulders, and stepped back, wiping off clumps of snow that had gathered on his coat. "Evil spirits flee when they see the sign of the cross. The power of Christ is too much for them."

"Evil spirits? I can't believe what I just saw." Jayden shook his head, contemplating. "If the cross felled the spirit, it makes sense why she left you alone. But why me? She could have torn me apart as she did Luice."

Savrin shrugged, stuffing the cross necklace back into his pocket. "Perhaps there is a greater destiny awaiting you. Either way, you should thank the Lord you are protected. Now, let's go." He continued the way they had been going, toward the mountain peak.

Jayden wanted to tend to Luice's body, but what could he do? They couldn't bury him, nor could they carry the extra mass. What they should have done was return to the port. They had no guide, and the strange event, was a bad omen. This Lord Hardwin had to have known of these dangers, which was why he sent others to accomplish this mission for him.

Against his best judgment, Jayden hurried after Savrin. "This is a bad idea." Even with the spirit gone, he couldn't help an eerie feeling of being watched—and not by a benevolent God protecting them.

* * *

JAYDEN AND SAVRIN ascended the remainder of the mountain without their guide. It made Jayden nervous. Though it was clear the direction they had to go—toward the summit—not knowing the specifics of the terrain could lead to disastrous pitfalls. What if wild animals came upon them? Or the snow obscured some pit which could make them fall? No one would be able to rescue them.

Luice had told them there were caverns to provide shelter ahead, but Jayden could see no sign of them in the blankets of whiteness all around. The best course would be to turn back and abandon their quest.

"I strongly advocate against continuing," Jayden said. "We should go back, see if we can bury Luice, and perhaps find another guide."

"Lighten up. We can handle this," Savrin said. He showed no signs of slowing his pace.

Jayden gripped Savrin by the arm to halt his progress. "Savrin."

"Hands off me!" Savrin shook his arm free.

"I've been more than patient. If this is some quest for treasure, and our food and lodging are being taken care of, it can wait. A day or two won't matter."

Savrin's eyes flicked to the ground.

"There's something you're not telling me," Jayden said.

"Lord Hardwin isn't doing this just for treasure," Savrin said.

Jayden huffed. Something felt wrong about this expedition from the beginning. He had been right all along. His intuition rarely failed him. Ever since he'd had that strange dream, his life had been set on a path which was not of his own volition. And yet he still continued. Did he truly have any choice in the matter? "I figured as much. What's this about?"

"He is part of a group," Savrin said, reaching into his pocket and pulling out his cross again. "We are called the Church Vigilant. We are looking for signs of the end times. There's a prophecy about a great song which will soothe the land and stave off the apocalypse. A warrior trades his sword for a harp as an ancient evil sheds its bonds. Sounds a lot like someone I know."

Jayden threw his hands up. "This is some crazy world-is-ending theory? Besides. I don't have a harp."

"No, it's not like that at all. There are ancient texts that—"

"You have to be kidding me. I'm toiling through the heavy snow in a blizzard, dealing with some strange spirit creature because of your cult?" Jayden turned to head back down the mountain.

"Please. Don't go. I need your help." Savrin followed him.

"Give me *one* good reason."

"Money? You need it. To buy a new instrument, remember?" Savrin asked.

"There must be easier ways to make coin. I may not be welcome back in Hyrum or Tyril, but I'm sure someone in the Freelands can use sturdy hands." Even though from what he'd seen, the people here didn't trust those from the west. If he'd had any kind of luck keeping himself gainfully employed, he wouldn't have been here.

Savrin thrust his arm out, the cross dangling before his eyes. "Because of this. I was right about the spirit, how this sign would be the way to fell it, was I not?"

Jayden pushed the necklace out of his face. "It seemed that way." He stopped in his tracks.

Savrin exhaled. "Lord Hardwin is part of an order of monks. They claim to date back to the beginning of the world, descended from the first ancients. The Church Vigilant. The Holy City doesn't acknowledge them, but they have libraries of texts. You should see it. There are histories, philosophies, art... you have no idea. Strange devices lost to time. But I digress. My point is, there is a lot of verifiable information which leads me to believe this is true. And much like my faith in the Lord Jesus Christ..." he jiggled his chain, "I am sure this is very real. And very true."

"This is too much for me to process," Jayden said.

Savrin placed a hand on Jayden's shoulder. "You can feel it in your soul. Have a little faith. If not in what we're doing, in me. For old times?"

"As I recall, I was getting you out of trouble then," Jayden said.

"And you will again. That's the best part. Come on." Savrin motioned his head and turned back toward the mountain.

After several more hours of traversing, they reached an entrance to a cave.

The sky darkened, making it hard for Jayden and Savrin to see. They'd packed torches to navigate inside, but it would have given Jayden some comfort if they would have returned to daylight.

If their guide had lived, they might have made it to the location faster, without so much wandering, but now they were on their own.

The men lit their torches and entered the cave.

An opening large enough for at least five men stretched before them, a black blight amongst all of the white snow. Once they lit their torches, the view gave Jayden pause.

Fresh tracks from mud and snow littered the entrance of the cave. At least two sets of them, though the way they stepped blended and became lost as they went along. The tracks had three toes and were three times the size of a man's foot.

Jayden pointed to the set of footprints. "What are we dealing with?

Beasts live in here. We should abandon this foolishness and come back with more men."

Savrin frowned. "I don't think there's time. We've already wasted too much."

"Your lord's strange premonition could surely wait a day or two," Jayden said.

"I wouldn't risk it."

Jayden shook his head. "You're going to get me killed."

"Not if I'm right," Savrin said. "Come on."

Savrin led the way inside, and they wound through a cavern with jagged rocks protruding from the walls. Something on the rock had rusted long ago, and Jayden stopped to look at a glimmering portion of the wall shining through a layer of dust. He rubbed his hands on it. The glimmering object was smooth, an onyx color. Above it was a carved symbol of some sort, a circular line with a sphere inside and another line making a point. It appeared to be a symbol, but he couldn't ascertain much else.

This was a wonder of the ancients. Jayden knew little about the old race, but legends told of their great creativity. The Holy City and its priests claimed they had been agents of God, but much detail had been lost to antiquity.

The onyx wall covering didn't aid them in their current quest, and so Savrin and Jayden continued on into the cave, which wound and broke into two paths. Jayden wished there were still tracks present to see which way the creatures may have gone, so they could stay far away and go the opposite direction.

"Which way do we go?" Jayden asked.

Savrin produced a copper coin. "Heads, left. Tails, right."

Not able to think of a better method to choose which way to go, Jayden shrugged.

Savrin flipped the coin.

It hit the ground, bouncing, and then landed softly on the dusty floor. Savrin crouched to pick the coin up. "Tails. We go right."

They continued onward. The cavern seemed to have several doors lining it, but each they tried refused to open, sealed shut from thousands of years of neglect. It would take more than a battering ram to get through those metals. Jayden wondered if every door would be subsequently closed to them. What if they couldn't find any of the ancients' treasures? This danger could have all been for naught.

Savrin seemed undeterred. He kept going, checking every door along the way.

A croaking sound came from deeper in the cavern. It echoed. Impossible to tell which way it came from.

"The creatures," Jayden breathed. His heart raced.

"We must be close to something big," Savrin said.

"You can say that again," Jayden said. He doubted it was anything good.

The flame from Savrin's torch flickered, the corridor seeming to dim. "The air's stale in here," Savrin said.

Jayden spotted a dark spot down the hallway. "Is that an open door?"

Savrin moved to the place Jayden pointed. His eyes brightened as he turned back to Jayden. "It is! Hold my torch. I'm going to have to squeeze through."

Jayden grabbed hold of the torch and Savrin set his pack down and pushed in the opening. The door was only about a third ajar, and the inside was pitch black. It took the rogue a few moments to make it through, leaving Jayden in the hallway alone.

"Torch." Savrin held his hand through the opening expectantly.

Jayden returned the torch to his companion.

"Look what we have here!" Savrin said.

"What is it?" Jayden peered through the opening. On the other side was a square room, not too big, with two bunk beds with a lot of dust on them, a dresser with dusty framed objects atop it, and a chest. There appeared to be a small opening on the other side of the room, but Jayden couldn't get a good look from his position to see where it led.

"There's hanging clothing. Strange attire," Savrin said, disappearing toward the opening. He coughed. "So dusty! I wonder if these would have any value."

"I'm sure 'the clothes of the ancients' could be used as some kind of attraction, at least. Any information about your great prophecy?" Jayden asked glibly.

"Don't be rude."

A padding *thud thud thud* came from further in the depths. Jayden turned back. Something cast a shadow. A big one.

It had to have been the creature which made the tracks.

Not waiting for the monster to find him, Jayden, dropped his pack and jammed into the opening. As he did, the creature came into view. As tall as the ceiling or taller crouching down, it had hunched over shoulders and greyish-green skin, with arms reaching to the floor like an ape. An ogre—or something like one of legend. Teeth protruded from its bottom jaw and it let out a guttural roar when it spotted Jayden.

"Lord," Jayden said, trying to squeeze further into the crack. His years of inactivity had left him out of fighting shape, and he struggled to fit. "Savrin, help me!"

"What's going on over there?" Savrin asked.

Jayden held his torch into the hallway and his free arm toward Savrin. "Grab my arm. Pull me in. Quickly!

The ogre rushed him, pounding its fists on the floor before reaching up to grab Jayden's arm. Savrin grabbed ahold of Jayden's free arm and tugged. It wasn't enough to force him through.

"Harder!" Jayden said.

"I'm going to rip your arm off," Savrin retorted.

"If you don't, this thing outside surely will."

"What thing?" Savrin glanced upward. His eyes went wide. "Oh."

Sweat dripped down Jayden's face. The ogre swatted at him, but couldn't get its hand in the cracks. Jayden let his arm fall to his side, the flame from the torch close to his body. Any closer and it would burn him.

Savrin kept pulling, and Jayden could feel himself slipping through to the other side. It was slow, and the wall and door scraped against his body painfully.

The ogre roared again. Its fingernail pushed into Jayden's arm as it tried to get its large hands into the crack.

Jayden yelped in pain. He pushed the torch outward toward the ogre. Soon, the smell of burning, rotting flesh filled the air.

The ogre took a moment to respond, its reaction delayed in backing away from the torch. Then, it howled from pain, its eyes shut and mouth open toward the ceiling. When it reopened its eyes, they glowed with a beady redness they hadn't had before.

"I think I just made it mad! Hurry," Jayden said.

Savrin gave one last tug and Jayden popped free of the doorway. He stumbled inside, but kept his torch upright.

The ogre outside pawed at the door, pushing its fingers inside.

Jayden glanced around the room. He'd seen most of it from outside, but now the extra area Savrin had mentioned came into view. It was a small hole in the back, filled with dusty hanging clothes. The ones Savrin had shaken the dust from had vibrant blues and reds. Dyes Jayden had never seen before. "Quite the ensemble."

The ogre pounded at the door, rattling the room.

"How are we going to get back out of here?" Jayden asked.

"We'll think of something," Savrin said.

Savrin opened one of the dresser drawers, dust puffed around him as he did so. He fanned the dust away as he found several strange objects, parchments, and other items which made little sense to Jayden.

"What are those?" Jayden asked.

"Who knows? Maybe you're right and we should have brought an entire team here to sort through these," Savrin said.

"Of course I was right." Jayden crossed his arms.

One of the strange objects was flat and had the same onyx surface Jayden had spotted on the walls outside. Was this some sort of gem the ancients adorned themselves with? It was difficult to see what use the flat object could have. Perhaps they used it as a board to cut on, but then, it didn't seem to have any scratches.

The ogre continued to paw at the door. It rattled, and Jayden turned. The creature had moved the door, only mere inches, but it had slid nonetheless. It wasn't giving up, and it seemed determined to get inside. "Savrin."

"Hmm?"

"You should turn around."

Savrin stepped to Jayden's side. "Oh."

"We're running out of time," Jayden said, brushing past his friend to rifle through the dresser drawers. He couldn't find anything of use inside. He had a knife, but it was in his backpack, which he'd dropped past the door. Beyond that, he didn't carry any weapons. He was trying to be a musician now and avoid violence.

Savrin apparently held no such convictions. He had a long blade in hand, which he swiped at the ogre from a safe distance. His attack missed. The ogre growled at him. The move barely slowed the creature down, and Savrin couldn't get in good enough range to be accurate against the creature. The door creaked as the ogre managed to slide it another inch.

These drawers were useless. The clothes hanging were useless. What else could he do?

One place in the room remained where Jayden hadn't explored—the chest.

He slid over to the chest, tugging at the top of it. A lock was on it, but it had rusted over. Jayden lifted his boot and brought it down hard on the lock. The rusted chain jiggled, but didn't break. He needed a tool, something harder. A thought dawned on him.

The door slid even further open, the ogre able to extend its entire arm through and squeeze some of its body in the door. If it used its full body weight, it would bust through with no problem.

Savrin flailed with his blade, but backed further away from the ogre's reach. "I'm going to stab it. If I don't survive, it was nice knowing you."

"Hold on," Jayden said. He grabbed the onyx pad from the dresser and rushed over to the chest. Clutching the pad with both hands, Jayden brought it down hard on the rock. The pad splintered, revealing smaller, shining objects inside. He kept slamming it down on the lock repeatedly.

The lock snapped off.

Jayden popped open the chest, revealing stacks of clothes and other items inside. He rummaged through it and found the clothes covered a hard object. Tugging on it, he could tell the object was heavy.

The clothes slipped off of it, revealing a gold, stringed instrument —a harp. It drew Jayden to it, as if it had some other-worldly property to it. For the first time, he believed Savrin's talk about destiny. Could this have been it?

"I need help over here!" Savrin shouted, breaking Jayden's reverie.

The ogre flung the door open and entered into the enclosure. Its giant frame barely fit, but it could still push through.

What could Jayden do? He couldn't fight it without heavy weaponry. It'd take a whole infantry unit with chainmail and lances to take that thing down.

"We have to lure it further in and run," Jayden said.

"Obviously," Savrin said, continuing to swipe at the ogre's arm with his meager knife.

The ogre burst through the door, losing its footing.

"Now's our chance. Hurry!" Savrin said.

Jayden hesitated. He needed the harp. Instead of running, he grabbed onto the harp. It was heavy as he expected and would slow him down.

Savrin made it to the other side of the ogre, which now loomed before them. It turned to face Jayden and roared at him.

He was trapped. There was no way he could avoid the creature's clutches.

"You idiot," Savrin said.

"You're the one who led me here," Jayden spat.

The ogre lunged toward him. Savrin, bless him, attempted to distract the ogre by swiping at its back with the knife. He broke skin, green blood oozing from the ogre's wound as it turned to face Savrin.

Jayden took the opportunity to move, his hands falling upon the strings of the harp as he did so. They were out of tune, and they made strange sounds, but still pleasant, as it was difficult to make an unpleasant sound come from a harp. He'd played one a few times before, back when he was in his home village as a youth. An old crone who lived down the street played one well, and she let him touch it sometimes, as she taught the children how to play the gittern and other instruments.

The ogre recoiled as if it were stabbed. Each pluck of the harp string tortured the creature's ears. It clawed at its own head, growling. Finally, the ogre stumbled, giving Jayden time to sneak to the other side of the room behind Savrin.

Savrin backpedaled toward the door, the ogre lashing out and flailing its arms. If its sharp nails struck, it would be deadly. "Hurry!" Savrin shouted.

Jayden didn't move. He had the harp. It was effective against this thing, strangely. He plucked a soft tune, the melody of a children's song that reminded him of holding hands as a youth and running in circles. Though the notes weren't in tune, they rang close enough to the semblance of music.

The ogre convulsed once more, roaring once more as it seemed to lose its bearings in the room. Its eyes glazed over as if drunk.

Determined, Jayden played the tune again, rhythmically, lulling in a mantra.

On the fifth pass through the instrumental pattern, the ogre collapsed to the floor unconscious. It breathed, though slowly.

Savrin touched the ogre with his toe. "That was amazing."

'We need to go," Jayden said.

Savrin grinned. "Yes. We do. This is what we came for. Not all this other stuff, though. I'll stuff a few of these ancient clothes into my pack and sell them. This harp is what we came here for. I can sense it now. Can't you?"

Jayden took a deep breath, surveying the ogre, and then the harp. He had connected to it, and with the way it had knocked the creature out, he had to admit the harp had properties beyond what he'd expected. "I suppose I do."

Savrin collected as much of the ancients' gear as he could carry, and he and Jayden vacated the cave. They picked up their pace, not wanting to risk the ogre awakening again, and exited into the night sky.

The clouds had cleared, leaving the moon large on the horizon, lighting their path on the white snow. It was colder than the day, their breaths lingering in the air as smoke even longer than before, but the harp radiated a warmth under Jayden's arm which helped to mitigate the chill.

Something crossed the moon in the sky—strangely, the shape he would expect of a dragon. "Did you see that?" Jayden asked.

"What?" Savrin asked.

When Jayden blinked, the image was gone. It had to have been his imagination. After this strange harp of the ancients had done something almost magical, his mind must have been playing tricks on him. "Nothing," he finally said.

The men traversed back to town, with Savrin boasting the whole time of his strange prophecies coming true.

## 2

Jayden strummed his harp in the common area of the Purple Tree Inn, a place in which he asked the innkeeper where it got its name, and the man shrugged and told him, "after a purple tree."

Ask a stupid question…

The thought distracted his musical efforts, causing a foul note to twang in the middle of his song. Jayden couldn't afford not to concentrate on the instrument. The harp proved to be much harder to handle than the gittern. Moreover, he hadn't had enough experience playing the harp, though his general proficiency with music made it easier to pick up than when he had first attempted the gittern. If only he had paid more attention in those old crone's lessons as a lad.

"Boo!" Savrin shouted, slamming a mug of beer down on the bar top. The commotion should have caused the other fifteen patrons in the place to turn and pay attention, but they seemed lost in their own worlds and conversations.

It was for the better. Jayden didn't want to draw anyone's focus. He needed to blend in as he reacquainted himself with the instrument, to be a part of the background ambiance. Once Savrin had a few drinks, his task became much more difficult.

"Play us *Echoes of Elvay!*" Savrin shouted.

The song he requested was a standard back in Hyrum, and instinctively, Jayden winced. Living in enemy territory, he'd become used to anything culturally Hyrum provoking a fight, but the Freelanders didn't seem to be offended by the choice in tunes. They had little awareness of any conflict going on between the two nations in the western half of the world.

The other patrons went back to their conversations and paid Savrin little heed. The bearded rogue had a jolly grin on his face, happy to have the attention. Jayden rolled his eyes.

Nonetheless, he played the song Savrin requested, a somber mid-tempo tune which would rise in intensity as the song progressed.

The harp came from the ancients the ancients, lasting these thousands of years concealed in a chest in a cave to the northwest of town, where they had hoped to find great wonders, but came up nearly empty other than the musical instrument. The harp itself had to have been worth hundreds of gold marks, but he couldn't bring himself to sell it. He had an attachment to the instrument, as if it spiritually bonded to him. Other than the harp, they'd brought back the ancient clothing—but when they tried to sell them to the merchants in town, no one believed their authenticity.

It left them without money for passage back. Savrin had counted on them having treasures to peddle for said journey, another detail he'd forgotten to tell Jayden. In the meantime, they were stuck working odd jobs. At least Jayden could attain work playing music. It beat manual labor.

Jayden continued plucking and singing throughout the evening, and he noticed something odd compared to the prior inns he'd played in—the patrons didn't leave. They stayed engaged with one another, at least superficially, but they appeared entranced, unable to move. Something smelled funny here.

When he ended his set, he took a seat at Savrin's table.

"You're not the best musician," Savrin said.

"I'm rusty with a harp." Jayden crossed his arms.

"Sure. I think we're going to need you to get better fast if you're gonna get tips enough to get us passage home," Savrin said. "How much did you make anyway?"

"No tips," Jayden said, frowning.

"None?!" Savrin slammed his hand on the table a little too loudly. The bar rattled, and he blinked. He then leaned in and lowered his voice. "None?"

"None. I'm not proud of it, but surely I wasn't that bad."

Savrin grimaced. "No, you should have gotten something." He glanced around. "There's something strange here. No one seems engaged at all. It's like we aren't even here."

Jayden noticed the patrons' strange mannerisms as well. He waved at a man at the closest table. No matter how hard he tried, he couldn't get the man's attention. "Everything's strange in these Freelands. I want to get out of here."

"We could maybe pick their pockets if they won't pay attention to us," Savrin said.

Jayden shot him a cold look. "Doesn't your moral code speak against such things?"

"A man needs to eat. We'll be forgiven. That's how salvation works." Savrin made a sheepish face.

"We're not thieves."

"Speak for yourself."

Jayden huffed. "*I'm* not a thief." He moved to pack up his harp while the innkeeper cleaned the bar. Soon, it was well past closing, and Jayden went to the innkeeper to get his pay.

The innkeeper didn't seem to notice him at the bar.

"Hello?" Jayden asked.

The innkeeper went about his work. Savrin came up beside Jayden, cocking his head. "They're not even living. It's like something is controlling them."

"Maybe something is," Jayden said.

The innkeeper opened a hatch which led to steps underground—a cellar, too dark for Jayden to see far into it. Several of the patrons followed the innkeeper down the steps. They formed a line, soldier-like in the way they processed forward. One by one, they disappeared into the cellar.

Jayden maneuvered around the bar, harp under his arm. He wasn't about to leave it behind. Something gave him pause.

"Where are you going?" Savrin asked.

"To see what's down below. Come on," Jayden said. He walked down the steps.

Savrin jogged behind him. "I thought you said I was the one rushing into dangerous situations."

* * *

THE STAIRWELL OPENED into an underground cavern, dark except for a flickering light of fire at the end, where it opened into a larger room. There, all the patrons gathered to listen to droning music, which didn't sound like it came from a stringed instrument.

Jayden peeked beyond the gathered crowd, tight in the corridor as the inn patrons moved slowly toward the sound, but saw nothing. When they arrived in the larger room, the innkeeper and patrons gathered around an organ up against a side wall. Pipes protruded from it, made of bone, which created the odd sounds. A pedal depressed to the floor, squeaking each time it moved and blew air through the instrument. But the odd part was—no one played it.

The keys of the organ moved themselves, the pedals depressing with no foot upon it. The sounds enthralled the patrons, their eyes wide and focused on the music. The innkeeper led them forward and all of them brought various coins from the Freelands forth to the organ, setting them atop of it in a jar.

"What by Jove is going on here?" Savrin asked. He pushed forward. "I haven't had enough to drink for this."

"I have had nothing to drink," Jayden said.

Savrin glanced over his shoulder. "Bar probably is open for the taking."

"We're not stealing alcohol," Jayden said.

"Spoilsport," Savrin said.

"What does your Church Vigilant say about your thievery?"

The question shut Savrin up.

Savrin and Jayden made their way through the room, but the patrons kept ignoring them, no matter where they stood. It was all too odd.

The enthralled customers lined in front of the organ, each depositing their coin. The jar soon filled to the brim with coppers and silvers, an eye-opening amount, to say the least. Jayden wished he could have made a quarter of the amount of coin on a good evening. He stepped forward to get a better look at the jar.

A wind rushed over him, keeping him back from the organ. It chilled through his bones, unnatural, much like they had experienced during their blizzard hike. It couldn't have come from anywhere in this cellar—but then, an organ shouldn't have been playing itself, either. There had been too many strange occurrences as of late in Jayden's life. He longed for a simpler time of playing his gittern in the streets of Tyril, busking for coin. Why had he ever let Savrin talk him into this strange adventure?

Savrin cocked his head at Jayden, looking at him like he was crazy. He made for the tip jar himself, but the force pushed him back as it had Jayden a moment prior.

"Whoa," Savrin said.

"Indeed," Jayden said. He pressed a hand forward and the same wall of wind kept him from approaching the organ.

Two spirits slithered from the top of the pipes. They appeared like smoke, small holes where the eyes and mouths should be. They swirled in the air, casting a shadow below.

"I think we woke something up," Savrin said.

"Get your cross," Jayden said.

Savrin already had the necklace in his hand, holding the cross up toward the apparitions.

Music continued to play, the patrons giving their tips. They moved in an orderly ritual, like some kind of religious ceremony. It had to be the music that kept them in such a trance, but why didn't it affect Jayden and Savrin?

The spirits hovered around Jayden. They'd taken notice of him and his colleague. These didn't have a corporeal form, but generated their wind energy to keep Jayden off balance.

Savrin jiggled his cross at the spirits, but unlike the one they'd fought in the past, the cross seemed to have little impact on the spirits attacking them now. "It's not working," Savrin said.

"Why not?"

"Don't know. Maybe they aren't evil?"

"They seem evil to me." Jayden kept trying to move forward.

Though the spirits had tremendous energy to them, he had the willpower to push his way to the organ. Each step took an eternity as he forced himself forward, inching closer to the instrument. The spirits spun around him even more strongly, trying to make one last effort to knock him down.

Jayden lost his footing, but Savrin was just behind him and kept him upright by gripping his arm. "I've got you," he said.

"Thanks," Jayden said. His hair blew in his face and his eyes watered from the sheer force the spirits created, but he was close enough to the organ to touch it. The song continued to play, the pedals still moving. The patrons kept emptying their pockets into the tip jar. Should he just wait until they were finished and they all left?

No, he wouldn't want them to lose their money because some spirit robbed them. Was this some plan of the innkeeper?

All he could think of to do was to play a song himself. If he interfered with the tune, it could break the trance, couldn't it? "I need you to get on the floor," Jayden said.

"Huh?" Savrin asked.

"I doubt I can man the pedals myself with these spirits, but I can reach the notes."

"You're going to play?" Savrin blinked.

"Can you follow orders for once?" Jayden asked, a little more curtly than he'd intended. He maintained his focus, however, willing his arms forward past the wall of energy the spirits made. His hair stood up on his arms as the wind kept blowing, but his strength surpassed the spirits'. It had been a while since Jayden had played a keyed instrument, but he could remember the basics. Jayden played the melody to a song he'd first learned when he'd entered service for Tyrim. *The Warrior's March.* It was a lively tune, meant to inspire the rank and file into higher morale. He hoped it would be enough to break the trance of the people here.

Despite Savrin's glib nature, he knelt on the ground, his hands moving the pedals as Jayden played. They worked as a team together.

He played the melody, and it interfered with the one the spirits were putting forth, creating dissonance in the room. The sound was jarring, and eventually, the spirit song stopped, while Jayden continued to play his tune. The wall of energy around him dissipated as well, the spirits howling soundlessly. They shot around the room wildly. The patrons woke from their trance at the same time, many voices asking how they had gotten in this strange cellar.

Dust plumed in the cellar from the spirits' frantic movement, but soon the spirits dissipated. They pulsed as they faded and eventually winked out of existence.

"What happened here? Did you put us under some sort of spell?" one patron asked, still holding his hand out over the tip jar.

"They were trying to steal our money," another said.

Jayden held his hands up in surrender. "No. You were entranced. We came here and broke the spell. I swear it."

Savrin scurried to his feet, as if expecting a fight. The angry patrons gathered around them, keeping them boxed in. *No good deed goes unpunished.* Perhaps Savrin had been right, and they shouldn't have interfered here.

Still, it was the right thing to do. Whether or not these people accepted it, he had done the moral thing.

The thought didn't bring him comfort as the patrons cornered him and Savrin. Why wouldn't they listen?

Suddenly, the innkeeper burst forward, pushing his way through the crowd of assembled patrons. "No! You're making a mistake. I promise, these men had nothing to do with your bewitchment."

The first patron narrowed his eyes. "Why do you say that?"

The innkeeper looked between the crowd, Jayden, and Savrin, and then he lowered his head, his shoulders drooping. "Because it was my fault."

Jayden cocked his head curiously at the innkeeper.

"My wife used to play the organ at The Star of the Sea church," the innkeeper said.

Another patron nodded. "I remember. She played softly. It was nice."

The innkeeper frowned, years of memories painted on his face. "When she passed, the church let me have her organ. I constructed a shrine to her down here, below my inn. I buried her here and hoped they would bury me beside her one day. A few days later, her spirit began playing. I missed the sweet sound and could feel her presence, so I encouraged it with incense and brought in a local shaman to amplify the spirit…" He shook his head. "It had the reverse effect, and another spirit joined with my wife, amplifying her power."

"It's never good to encourage spirits," Savrin said. "They must go forth on their journey."

Jayden played a chord on the organ keys. "Everyone here was entranced, but we weren't. I wonder why?"

An older man came forward. "I can answer that. I'm the shaman of whom he speaks."

The gathered crowd muttered to each other. None seemed to be comfortable with the idea of magicks.

"All here save for you two took communion with the church where she played. You were all connected," the shaman said, pointing to the crowd.

"I suppose that makes sense," the innkeeper said. He grabbed the tip jar. "I apologize for the inconvenience, fair travelers. I know you were working my inn to pay for passage home, and you have saved us. I hope this will cover the amount."

Savrin took the jar into his hands. "You're quite generous."

The patrons didn't seem too happy, but none protested. They had been entranced, and likely would have remained that way if it weren't for Jayden. He'd done some good here, but he desperately wanted to get out of these strange Freelands, where supernatural occurrences appeared to be much more regular than he could have fathomed mere weeks ago. Jayden couldn't wash his hands of this business fast enough. He'd never encountered spirits before he'd come to this land, but he had an uneasy feeling they'd be following him no matter where he traveled.

# INTERLUDE

Interlude

Jayden leaned over the railing on the bow of the trading vessel. He and Savrin had scraped enough from the coin the innkeeper had given them for passage on the first ship available, finally getting them out of the Freelands and on their way back to Kabak, a coastal city in Hyrum. While still technically exiled from Hyrum, Jayden didn't worry about returning. Few would recognize him anymore, and he could cross the border into Tyril if anything went wrong.

He sighed with a sense of relief while considering the future. The Freelands had brought him nothing but headache, and it could have been much worse of a journey had they not been lucky. He would have done anything to be away from all of those spirits and strange occurrences.

Savrin slouched onto the railing beside him. "The sea is beautiful, is she not?"

Jayden shrugged. "I wasn't much thinking about it."

"What were you thinking about, then?"

"Home."

Savrin paused, staring out toward the waves, the soft early evening sunlight reflecting a pinkish color off them. "Hyrum hasn't been home in a long time."

"No, it hasn't."

"Do you miss it?" Savrin tilted his head at Jayden.

Jayden frowned. "Sometimes. Ever since Huldra…"

He shook his head. He didn't want to think about her anymore. Those days were long since past.

Wind picked up, beating against the large sail in the center of the ship, causing it to flap, and some of the merchant seamen tightened the ropes to make sure it stayed put. It was a good distraction from his thoughts. He didn't want to think of Huldra. Her beautiful blonde hair, her round face, her caring and devoted eyes…

Jayden pushed himself from the railing.

"Where are you going?" Savrin asked.

He shrugged. "To find something to eat. Let's talk about what we're going to do when we get back. I want to meet this Lord Hardwick."

The two men made their way below decks.

# 3

THE MARKETS IN KABAK WERE THINLY POPULATED, BUT JAYDEN FOUND some bread rolls and berries so he would have something to eat for the evening, before they journeyed to meet Savrin's friend Lord Hardwick. As they came closer, the talk of the various towns was of prophecy from the Church Vigilant. It seemed Savrin wasn't the only one caught up in these stories.

Kabak was a city made of old stones, with moss growing between many of them. Much of it hadn't been cleaned in recent days, grime building on the dark stone along all the buildings. Half of the structures appeared to be vacated, and some remained broken down into rubble from the warring with Tyril, when catapults from the sea had bombarded the city.

As a consequence, merchants had all but abandoned the place, with bare markets for a city of such a size. Only a few patrons strolled through the stalls.

Jayden returned to the inn, tucking his cloth-wrapped food under one arm, and opening the door with his other hand. He expected to see Savrin inside, already helping himself to the common bar, but a surprise greeted him instead.

Four men stood in their battle armor, helmets and all, swords brandished. One of them held a point of a sword to Savrin's neck, as forcing him to kneel. A crimson sash across the chest marked the commander of the soldiers, and he paced back and forth until his attention moved to the door—and to Jayden.

A wry smile ticked upward on the commander's face, matching the curve of his mustache. "Well, well. Jayden, traitor to the empire. As I live and breathe," he said.

"Commander Brim," Jayden said. He recognized the man from his unit, the one he had defected from because of its brutality. Of course, Brim would have been promoted in the intervening time. Recalling Brim's savage acts toward civilian women—it made Jayden's fist clench. But he couldn't take on four armed soldiers, not even if he'd had a weapon on him. It surprised him, however, that these soldiers greeted them so quickly. It had been years since he'd been here. How could they have been on the lookout so readily?

"I heard from a friendly seaman that you had made your way back into this country. You should have known better. We don't look kindly on defectors," Brim said. He stepped forward and pressed the point of his sword against the right side of Jayden's breast. "You shouldn't have come back."

Jayden frowned. He probably should have protested coming to Hyrum, but he couldn't have anticipated anyone from his old border unit being in town. No one should have recognized him here. There was no strategic value to the place—except, on second thought, it might be exactly the place they would station troublemakers who the Sorcerer King wanted out of the way. "Perhaps not. But we were just passing through. There aren't many ships traveling to this side of the world from the Freelands. Let Savrin go and we'll be on our way."

Brim laughed, digging the sword point a little more into Jayden's shirt and flesh.

Jayden tried not to wince.

"No, I'm afraid that won't be possible this time," he said. "Bind him," he instructed to two of his men.

The two soldiers rushed over to Jayden, pulling his arms behind him and causing him to drop his food on the floor. The bread rolled across the room. The soldiers wrapped ropes—made from a harsh, prickly material—around his wrists, tight against his skin.

Jayden struggled, but it did no good. There was little he could do with the sword pointed at him and two soldiers manhandling him. "There's no reason for this," Jayden said.

"Ah, but there is," Brim said, motioning to Savrin. The men bound him along with Jayden and forced them to stand. "You'll come with us, and we'll see what the Sorcerer King has to say about traitors. I gather his punishment would be much worse than what I'd do with you, were it my decision." He made a motion across his own throat as if he were slitting it. "At least my methods are quick and merciful."

Jayden recalled them being anything but, with the way Brim had treated innocents, but he kept his lips shut. Taunting the man wouldn't do him any good.

While Jayden considered his options, Savrin broke his binds with his pocket knife and bolted for the door. He caught the soldiers flat-footed with his resistance. Jayden stuck a leg out to trip one of them as he chased after Savrin. The soldier collapsed to the floor.

Savrin burst through the door and slammed it shut behind him before the guards could collect themselves.

Brim grabbed Jayden by the shirt and pulled him close, his breath smelling of fish and garlic. "That was foolish to injure my man."

"I don't know what you're talking about." Jayden held his head high, defiant.

Brim slapped him across the face. Jayden's head whipped to the side. "We'll see how disrespectful you'll be when you get in front of the Sorcerer King. One prisoner is as good as two," he grumbled. "Now move."

The soldiers led Jayden out of the inn and toward the castle on a hill in the middle of town.

* * *

THE GUARDS BROUGHT Jayden to the steps of the Sorcerer King's castle, a piecemealed building, with new sections added onto several times over the years, towering over the city like a hulking monstrosity ready to swipe at the residents below. Stationary guards opened the doors, and those with Jayden pushed him inside.

Brim led the way, pacing confidently in victory over Jayden. If they had battled man-to-man, without the help of his goons, it would have been different.

Jayden shook his head at his thoughts. He wouldn't have wanted to do battle, even if it had been an option. Those days were better left in the distant past. He had his harp now—a dedication to music instead of violence—which he hoped would remain safe in the inn through whatever show trial Brim had in mind.

The soldiers guided him to the royal chambers, where they opened large double doors before a red carpet which ran like a river toward a red-carpeted dais with a golden throne set atop it. On the throne sat the Sorcerer King, regal, his head inclined. The Sorcerer King had a pronounced chin, accented by a dark beard, and cat-like eyes, narrow and vigilant. He wore a heavy purple robe lined with furs, and a golden crown atop his head.

Before him knelt a frail man, dressed in brown, tattered clothing—monks' robes. He had scraggly hair and a thin beard which fell upon his chest. He shook as he spoke. "Please, Sire. You must listen to me. I've had visions of what is to come."

"I'm not entirely certain how you were allowed entry to the palace," the Sorcerer King said.

"The Lord works in mysterious ways," the man in robes said.

The Sorcerer King flicked two fingers to the side, manipulating a strange force, causing the monk to fall sideways, prostrate on the ground. "We'll have no talk of vile superstitions here. I am your god now."

The monk shook his head, despite the Sorcerer King's warning. "No. Never. There is but one God. You are a pretender and you must renounce the world and your throne if you want to save this kingdom. Music will sound from the heavens. The great dragon will rise. The people will tremble with—"

The old man's words abruptly ended when the Sorcerer King lifted his hand and lightning flew from his fingertips. Electricity flowed through the man, and his eyes rolled back. The old man shook violently, his flesh burning from the raw energy, until he stopped moving and lay unbreathing.

"Remove him from the chamber," the Sorcerer King said.

Guards appeared from behind the side pillars to haul the remains of the old man away. They passed Jayden and the soldiers with him without so much as a glance.

The Sorcerer King closed his eyes and breathed, centering himself. Did he need to recover after expelling such power? The ruler's eyes opened again, settling upon Jayden. "What have we here?"

Brim sauntered forward before taking a knee before the Sorcerer King. "Sire, I bring you a boon."

"Oh?"

"The traitor Jayden, from my unit. We have found him and apprehended him," Brim said.

The Sorcerer King's eyes fell upon Jayden, scrutinizing him. "It has been a number of years since you fled your duties. You were going to be one of my top commanders. Such a shame," he said.

Jayden kept his mouth shut.

"Proud as ever," the Sorcerer King said, shaking his head. "Bring him before me."

The soldiers pushed Jayden forward.

"Kneel," Brim said.

Jayden held his ground.

Brim kicked him in the leg behind the knee and his legs buckled. "I said, *kneel.*"

Jayden collapsed on the step before the dais, his knees scraping against the carpets, still holding his head high. He would look his tormentor in the eye and would not cower. No matter what, he would remain dignified.

"Proud to the last, hmm?" the Sorcerer King asked. His eyes had an unnatural fire to them which chilled Jayden to his core. It was as if he weren't entirely human anymore. Something had corrupted his soul— the magicks. It had to have eroded whatever humanity had been there.

The last Jayden had seen the monarch, he had been a tyrant, but still a man. Someone with ambition, who wanted to piece together the western realms into one "Holy Empire" as he had called it then. It seemed times had changed since Jayden had gone into exile.

The Sorcerer King's eyes flicked to the side. "You be made an example of. No one defies my rule. This will be public, and it will be painful. Brim."

Brim stepped forward. "Yes, Sire."

"Place him in the dungeon and schedule an execution in the square at dawn tomorrow."

"Yes, Sire." Brim bowed his head. He motioned, and the soldiers took Jayden by the arms, lifting him back to his feet.

Jayden didn't remove his eyes from the Sorcerer King. He didn't fear evil. It hadn't when he had to defy his orders in the name of justice, and it wouldn't now. Nor did he fear death.

"I wish you would put your fire toward my cause," the Sorcerer King said.

"Your cause is devilry," Jayden said. He clamped his lips tight after uttering the words, instantly regretting them. Why had he taunted the Sorcerer King so? It wouldn't matter, he supposed. His execution would occur regardless. Getting the sole verbal jab in brought him some comfort.

The Sorcerer King raised his hands, sparks forming in them as they had with the old man before. Is this how the tyrant dealt with anyone who said something displeasing to him?

Jayden braced for immediate death, wincing.

The Sorcerer King let his hands fall and the sparks dissipate. "No. I will be patient. The world needs to see the result of defying me. Take him away."

The soldiers dragged Jayden out of the king's chambers and down steps leading to an underground dungeon.

* * *

THE SOUND of dripping water kept Jayden from sleeping. The whole dungeon had a murkiness to it, not cleaned in years, smelling of mold and death. The Sorcerer King paid little heed to the comfort of his prisoners.

Jayden had slept in worse conditions, back during his military deployment—mud, filth—he'd endured discomfort. Even so, sleep would not come this evening.

Impending death couldn't cause his lack of sleep either; it was a state he'd grown used to during his time in the military. Any battle could have been his last. Something about the way the old man had prophesized about the world bothered him more. Could there have been merit to his words? It fell in line with what Savrin had told him the Church Vigilant said. For the Sorcerer King to savagely kill him for bringing a warning...

Something slammed against the hard stone of the walls and broke Jayden's reverie. He inclined his head toward the bars of his cell—though in the dark he could see little.

Footsteps fell, echoing in the dungeon. They came ever closer. The Sorcerer King could have sent an assassin in the night, but then, why would he have worried about the public spectacle? Who else could be out there?

Keys jingled, and a silhouette materialized in front of the cell. A cloaked man. Eventually, he found the keys and placed them within the lock, turning and opening the door. He stepped forward and knelt before Jayden, then placed a key into his shackles, unbinding him.

Jayden wiggled his foot; the shackles around his ankle had caused it to lose feeling. Perhaps the tingling in his foot was why he couldn't achieve rest this evening. "Thank you?" he said, the question more directed at who this could be.

"No problem," came the voice of Savrin. He looked up and pushed back his hood. "You didn't think I'd leave you here, did you?"

Both Jayden and Savrin stood.

"I assumed you'd be long gone by now," Jayden said.

"Tsk, tsk," Savrin said, leading him out of the cell.

"How'd you get in here?" Jayden asked.

"I've got friends in the city. They're waiting to extract us," Savrin said.

Jayden followed Savrin to the steps leading back into the main palace. Darkness fell over all the rooms, furniture, vases, and tapestries, casting shadows in the rooms. No guards patrolled, at least for the time being.

Savrin brought a finger to his lips to warn Jayden to be quiet and carefully moved ahead, his footsteps creating no sound any longer. When the man wanted to be silent, he could make himself like a ghost.

They crept through a corridor which had several rooms branching off it—servants' quarters, judging by the size of them. One door held slightly ajar, something glowing from behind it. Jayden stopped. Something felt amiss here. He wanted to explore more and find out the reason an old prophet would draw such ire from the Sorcerer King.

"Keep going," Savrin whispered.

"There's something here," Jayden said.

"We don't have time."

"It might be important," Jayden said. His friend didn't have the patience he did. He pushed the door open to find a woman asleep on a slab in the middle of an empty room. Ancient symbols pulsed in a glowing light from the wall. The Sorcerer King's devilry on display.

For some reason, Jayden couldn't divert his attention from the woman. It took him a moment to realize why she compelled him. He recognized her—Princess Bronwyn. He hadn't seen her in years, but she hadn't aged since he could recall seeing her. Long, blonde locks flowing down her back, and wearing a gown of white, she looked peaceful in her slumber, like an angel. Her hands were folded over her stomach, and her breasts rose and fell shallowly with each breath. She lived, at the very least.

Savrin tugged at Jayden's sleeve. "I don't know what you're trying to accomplish—is that the princess?" His vocal tone changed mid-thought to surprise.

"It is," Jayden said.

"It's not our problem. We have to—"

Jayden pushed Savrin back and stepped toward the princess. Her beauty captivated him like none other, save his old flame Huldra. Princess Bronwyn had been of the royal family before the Sorcerer King came to power. He had been regent then, but had seized power. None in Hyrum saw it coming until he had the palace guard to himself. The rest of the royal family had died in mysterious accidents, but he claimed the princess had abdicated authority to him. Her presence confirmed what he'd said, but it had always felt wrong somehow.

Her body radiated light. Jayden leaned over her.

"What are you doing?" Savrin asked.

He couldn't be so sure himself. Something drew him to her, made him want to be closer to her. His heart beat with anticipation as he leaned in closer. She smelled of flowers, a scent as beautiful as her appearance. Further compelled, Jayden brushed his lips against hers.

They were soft, tender. If only he could have kissed her while awake.

Her eyes fluttered open, and then they went wide.

She tried to scream, but Jayden covered her mouth with a hand. He made the same motion with his finger as Savrin had to warn him to be quiet.

Her blue eyes bulged, but then calmed as she saw Jayden.

"I'm not here to hurt you. I'm here to take you out of here. Will you be quiet and come with us?" Jayden asked.

The princess nodded.

Jayden removed his hand from her mouth and then assisted her to her feet. She wobbled at first, apparently having lain there for a long time.

"What's happened?" she asked softly.

"I suspect the Sorcerer King had you under a spell. But we can consider what happened later. We have to get out of here," Jayden said.

"Follow me," Savrin said, motioning to them.

The three returned to the corridor. The princess only had her white dress and no shoes on her feet. It would make it difficult to traverse terrain outside, but her steps caused the least noise amongst them while in the palace.

They reached an entrance to the castle, and Savrin bade them to wait. He crouched, slowing his movements as he opened the door.

A guard stood on the other side and turned. Savrin flashed a knife into his hand and slit the guard's throat in a motion nearly too fast for Jayden to see. A second guard approached in short order, and Savrin made quick work of him, slitting his throat and letting the guard's body to fall atop the first.

Savrin took one guard's sword and held it toward Jayden.

Jayden shook his head. "I don't want one," he said.

"You'll take it, and you'll help if we need to. Our survival might depend on it," Savrin said.

Jayden grimaced but took the sword from his friend. "Fine."

Bronwyn stepped over the bodies and grabbed her own sword.

"Do you know how to use one of those?" Savrin asked.

"Pointy end toward the bad guys," Bronwyn said.

Jayden shrugged. "Good enough."

Savrin bounded down the steps. "Come on. We don't want to wait until someone finds out we're here."

* * *

THEY REACHED the edge of the city without incident, but it would take some doing to get past the gates. Several guards stood there, and the three of them looked about as suspicious as anyone could. More, no one should be running out of the city at this time of night. But they couldn't wait until morning to make their move.

Savrin kept them out of view of the guards, around the corner of a local shop.

"There's something we should go back for," Jayden said.

"Hmm?" Savrin asked.

"My harp."

Savrin shook his head. "My friends have already handled it. They took your instrument to their monastery earlier. You'll be able to retrieve it there."

Jayden relaxed his shoulders. Knowledge of the harp's safety brought him great comfort. The uncertainty of what had happened to it had grated on him since being captured. Perhaps that was why he couldn't sleep in the cell.

"What do we do?" Princess Bronwyn asked.

"We fight," Savrin said.

"There's at least six below and more up on the walls," Jayden said. "We won't be able to get past them."

"I can handle at least three before they spot us and sound the alarm," Savrin said.

Jayden grimaced. He did not doubt Savrin's abilities, but he also didn't want to engage in fighting himself. It had been so long since he had a true battle, but he would hold his own if he had to. If only it could be easier to renounce violence.

"On three, I'll go forward. Let me handle the first group, and then you come in after they've noticed," Savrin said.

Jayden nodded. He glanced at Bronwyn. She gripped her sword so tightly her knuckles turned white. Not only would Jayden have to face difficult odds in a fight, but he would have to protect her as well.

In the time he'd taken to scrutinize their new female companion, Savrin had already pushed ahead. He crouched in the shadows, almost to the first guards. A set of three on this side of the entrance to the city, and a set of three on the other.

The rogue moved like the wind. The first guard had his throat slit before he knew anyone was there. Savrin moved with discipline and precision, almost the same way he had handled the guards in the palace. The fluidity of his work came from years of experience.

The guard collapsed, gripping at his neck, but unable to call for help as Savrin severed his vocal cords.

Savrin moved onto the second, using the same maneuver again, going right for the throat. The third guard turned and saw what was happening to his companions.

"Alarm!" the guard shouted. It would draw the attention of the other three.

"Time to move," Jayden told Bronwyn.

He ran forward, charging with his sword. His movement distracted the third guard on this side of the wall long enough for Savrin to stab him, slicing upward through the man's chest. The guard crumpled to the ground like the others.

But three more came from the other side of the wall, prepared to fight them.

Worse, two watch tower guards atop the wall took notice of them. Arrows flew in their direction.

Thankfully, in the moonlight, the first volleys missed. But they couldn't fight out in the open for long, or they would fall prey to the projectiles.

The guards met Savrin and Jayden with swords drawn. Steel clashed against steel. Bronwyn hadn't made it to the fighting yet— probably for the better.

"Stay back," Jayden ordered, hoping she would listen.

The girl didn't listen, but kept moving tepidly forward.

Two of the guards had occupied Savrin, who blocked their blades with amazing speed. Jayden faced one, but was rusty from years of playing the gittern instead of practicing combat.

The guard was younger and stronger than Jayden. Each blow forced Jayden's arms back. He would lose a battle of attrition, but perhaps he could outsmart the guard.

Not with the arrows flying at him, though. One narrowly missed hitting his side and plowing into the ground below.

One guard pulled a maneuver to force the blade from Savrin's hand, disarming his friend.

Bronwyn foolishly rushed forward, her sword lifted with both hands over her head. No form, leaving herself open. If his own opponent hadn't occupied Jayden, he would have yelled at the girl.

But another hard blow from the stronger guard in front of him demanded his attention instead. As he worried about Bronwyn, he almost took a sword to the gut, narrowly avoiding getting slain. The guard sensed the combat momentum turning firmly in his direction and brandished a confident grin.

Savrin scrambled for his blade while Bronwyn distracted the guards. When her steel met theirs, her blade flew from her hands.

This fight had been doomed from the start.

Another volley of arrows rained from above. This time, one came perilously close to Bronwyn. She let out a soft cry.

Jayden turned. It proved to be the wrong call.

The guard struck him in the arm, and he dropped his sword. Pain flared in his bicep. He wanted to scream, but it would do no good.

Regardless, the three of them were now disarmed, with the guards closing in on them and arrows trained from above.

Savrin, Jayden, and Bronwyn all backed away. It would do no good to run. They would be trapped in the city, and easily recognizable, especially with the girl in the white gown.

"Surrender yourselves," one guard said. "If our archers don't get you, we can cut you down just as easily."

Jayden put his hands up. He saw no alternative. He would die anyway in the morning. Perhaps it would be better to go down in a fight. If he could trick the guards forward…

All heads turned as a scream came from above. An archer fell from the tower.

On the opposite side, another went down.

Jayden kicked the guard in front of him. The man to fell, dropping his sword.

Savrin did similar with the second guard, leaving only the third with a blade. The remaining guard swung at Jayden, forcing him back, the blade barely missing his belly.

"I don't know what you think you're doing, but—" The guard's words died in his throat as he gurgled. An arrow had hit him in the throat.

Did the archers miss?

Jayden peered toward the gate. A group of robed men had gathered, two archers aiming at the guards. The other two guards put their hands up as Jayden and Savrin grabbed their blades.

"My friends are here," Savrin said, pride in his voice.

"I can see that."

One of the robed men jogged forward. "We have horses. Run from the city and get on their backs."

"What are you going to do with the remaining guards?" Bronwyn asked.

Savrin had already slit one of their throats before anyone could answer. Jayden knocked the other in the head with the butt of his sword, causing the guard to lose consciousness.

They couldn't allow the guards to go summon their masters, but he didn't have to resort to murder, either.

Jayden dropped his bloody sword. "Let's go."

Bronwyn looked like she was about to retch, but she followed them to the horses.

## 4

JAYDEN AWOKE ON A SMALL COT IN A STRANGE ROOM. HE'D BEEN
sweating in his sleep, hands clutching to the sheets. Nightmares of the
Sorcerer King haunted him—the monarch vowing to hunt him down
and slay him. Had he truly drawn such ire from the man?

Given the circumstances of his escape, it could be worse now than
it had been when he'd confronted the tyrant.

A bowl of water waited on a dresser for him to freshen himself
with. Jayden put on his clothes to join the others outside.

His room opened to a courtyard, one with a serene landscape of
lawn, rocks, a fountain, and small trees. Beyond its walls, a cliff over-
looked the Holy City, where the church had set itself away from prin-
cipalities, conducting its own business. Though it lay directly between
Hyrum and Tyril, the city stayed out of the conflict.

Its inhabitants walked the streets, looking like mere ants from this
place atop the hill.

Jayden's room was but one of many in a row, quarters meant for
monks and guests of the monastery. A small chapel lay in the eastern
corner, and a mess hall and recreational area were on the other end.
The monks had tillable land on which they toiled, and a small brewery

where they crafted beer. Savrin finagled his way into sampling some when they arrived the prior evening. Jayden, tired from the evening's events and distraught by the violence, chose to retire instead.

His companions sat on a bench by the fountain, talking with two monks and a man dressed in fine silks. He had a pointed beard and a jolly look about him—a man who hadn't seen the horrors of war as Jayden had.

Jayden stepped to the group. "Good morning."

"Welcome back to the land of the living," Savrin said. He motioned to the people there. "These are my monk friends, brothers Menek and Jarrod, and I believe it's high time you met Lord Hardwick." With his last introduction, he pointed toward the finely attired man.

"Savrin's mentioned you," Jayden said, offering his hand.

Hardwick shook with a firm grip. "He's spoken to me of you as well. You retrieved the Harp of Ancients from the Freelands?"

"If that's what it is." Jayden glanced about. "Where is the harp?"

"In the room next to yours," Menek said. "It's being polished and cleaned to better serve you."

"Thank you," Jayden said, unsure of the proper way to respond.

It seemed to please the monk, who nodded.

"There are troubling times ahead," Hardwick said. "But we can talk of that later. You've had a hard enough a night. Did you know the brothers of the Dark Hill Monastery are some of the finest cooks in all the western lands? Come. You must be famished, and you deserve a good meal."

The group migrated into the mess hall, where they sat upon benches while the monks served them pancakes and cured meats. As Hardwick had expressed, the monks had an exquisite talent in their craft of food.

"We do all things for the glory of God," Jarrod told them. "We must perform our tasks to His standards."

It made sense to Jayden. He tried to take pride in everything he did as well.

The monks opened a book, a genealogy of ancestors, of which they were particularly interested in speaking about with Bronwyn. She could trace her lineage could back to the first ancients themselves. Her bloodline was unparalleled.

As one of the monks named Bronwyn's ancestors aloud, the place shook, like someone had pounded a fist against a thin wall. The plates rattled on the table, and everyone looked disturbed.

"A sign?" Savrin asked.

Hardwick frowned. "Perhaps. There are several signs and portents during these times, but we should not look into every natural occurrence as such. This is why the Church Vigilant exists, to take notice of such matters."

"We will pray over the matter," Jarrod said, inclining his head toward Menek. The monks seemed to communicate with the mere movement of their eyes and retired away from the rest of them, moving to a corner of the room and sitting in a lotus position, muttering.

The entire scene made Jayden uneasy. He didn't know Hardwick, save from Savrin's working for him. However, he couldn't distrust this Church Vigilant too much, as they had mounted a rescue of him from the Sorcerer King. "What's the plan from here? We can't stay in this monastery forever. I am no monk."

Savrin glanced to Hardwick for answers.

"You have a destiny to fulfill," Hardwick said.

"So I've been told, though I'm skeptical. I'm a simple man, a soldier no longer, but a musician. My destiny will be to play."

"It seems so."

The words sounded ominous, and with them came more strange signs. The skies darkened, casting a shadow on the entrance to the mess where the door was open. Most of the monks remained in prayer, but one broke off to shut the door. Jayden became curious as to what transpired outside. He flung his legs around the bench and jogged outside.

Dark clouds swirling in the atmosphere had covered the sun. A storm rose quickly, much more so than Jayden had ever seen. Rain fell on the Holy City, the waves along the shoreline rising to whitecaps and larger. They pelted the beaches, and soon came up to the walls of the lower city itself. A giant wave rose above the walls, splashing down below.

People screamed in the distance by the shoreline. The rain dumped from the sky. Winds gusted, blowing hard rain into Jayden's face. He retreated inside.

"I've never seen anything like it," Jayden said.

"The weather isn't right. It's the sign of the end of the age," Hardwick said.

"And this comes from prophecy?" Jayden asked.

Hardwick nodded. "We've deciphered some of the ancients' writings. This world is their devising. They caused the seas to form, the mountains to rise. How, I know not. Their ways were mysterious, though they brought with them the word of the Lord and our salvation through Christ Jesus."

"But they also brought something else," Menek said, having rejoined them from his prayer, along with several of his brothers. "Something evil. They didn't know it was within their midst."

"Where did they come from?" Jayden asked.

Menek shrugged. "Eden, perhaps. We have lost the information over time. Though what's not lost is the evil one who dwells within the earth. He is there, and it seems he breaks from his prison."

"It sounds like old stories to frighten children," Jayden said.

Savrin motioned to the door to the mess, rain pouring down like water from a giant pitcher in the sky. "Does this seem like a story to you? You've seen spirits and other unnatural things. These infernal beings would not be arising, or stuck within this realm, if there were not something holding them here."

Jayden considered. "Suppose you're right and suppose I take this on face value. What does this have to do with me?"

"I've read my scriptures," Hardwick said. "Perhaps I can illuminate some of them. The ancients were clear that songs of praise were important to keeping the demon within its prison. We have words, and perhaps we can find a pattern of chords for you to play on the harp. Savrin says you are a bard, of course. And you've already seen signs and wonders. We are not quick to say this prophecy is being fulfilled, but if it is, we need to be ready."

"We are still studying the ancient texts. Dark matters are coming upon us faster than we anticipated," Jarrod said.

* * *

THE STORM RATTLED THE WINDOWS. Water dripped from leaks in the tiles in the ceiling. It poured for hours, and didn't appear to be letting up. The monks, Hardwick, and Savrin huddled together among old books and scrolls, formulating a plan. The texts were in an ancient writ Jayden didn't understand, and so he left the monks to their devices while the weather raged outside.

Jayden paced nervously around the mess hall.

Bronwyn clutched a cup of steaming tea. "I wish you'd sit down," she said.

"Sorry," Jayden said, stopping and seating himself across from her.

A small smile formed on the corner of her lips. "Better."

"How are you faring?" Jayden asked. He had never been the best at small talk, preferring to focus on jobs at hand. His father worked with horses when Jayden was a youth, and spent long hours outside without many people around. Jayden often joined him until he enlisted in the service. If only the Sorcerer King hadn't pushed for war, his life might have been a peaceful one. Alas, fate had other plans for him. At least, if Savrin's words could be counted on to be true.

Jayden's eyes flicked to the rogue who appeared hard at study in the old texts. It surprised him. The rogue seemed so whimsical but Jayden understood the man could be deadly focused when he held deeper convictions. Though he had spent little time with Savrin in recent years, Jayden had deep trust for him. They had fought side by side through the most difficult of battles. Jayden would trust his life to the man.

Moreover, Savrin's faith had been so stalwart. The rogue had no doubt of fate or destinies. This wasn't some ploy for him to make some coin. Jayden had also seen enough strange wonders with his own eyes to know something stirred in the spiritual realms. What? He couldn't tell. At least not yet.

Bronwyn glowered at him.

Jayden blinked. "What?"

"You weren't listening to me."

"I was too."

"What did I say?"

Jayden's mouth hung agape, unable to think of an excuse.

"Exactly," Bronwyn said, crossing her arms over her chest. "Men."

"I didn't have to rescue you, you know," Jayden said.

"You came in to steal a kiss from me," Bronwyn said.

Jayden tensed. "You remember that."

"How could I not?"

An awkward silence fell between them. Jayden hadn't exactly intended on kissing her, but he'd become drawn to her, almost as if some force compelled him to do so. She had a radiance he'd never seen another woman—though, come to think of it, he hadn't confirmed anyone else seeing it about her. Perhaps it was his imagination playing tricks on him, his heart stirring in a way it hadn't since Huldra.

Jayden blinked twice.

"Is something wrong?" Bronwyn asked, more confused than angry.

Before he could respond, his attention turned to the gathered group in the corner.

"A demon shall arise!" Savrin slapped his hand on a table away from them. "This is what we're looking for."

"Do you think it means the dragons the merchants say are prowling around The Demon's Eye Lake?" Hardwick said.

"The lake must be named such for a reason," Savrin said.

Jayden shook his head. "This is too much for a simple warrior," he said, standing.

"Our conversation?" Bronwyn asked. Leave it to a female to make everything about her.

It would be better to not dignify her with a response. He made his way for the group. The men turned. "Pardon the interruption," Jayden said. "Savrin, you mentioned your friends secured my harp before leaving the city?"

"Ah, yes. It's stored in one of the guest quarters. The one by yours," Menek said.

"I shall retrieve it then," Jayden said.

"In this storm?" Savrin cocked a brow.

"I've got not much better to do. It will relieve the tension to play some music," Jayden said.

Savrin frowned. "Be careful."

"It's just a little rain," Jayden said. He bowed to the gathered crew and took his leave. Out of the corner of his eye, he couldn't help but sneak a glance at Bronwyn. She appeared disconcerted, though this entire situation was less than ideal. He couldn't blame her.

Another part of him wanted to wrap his arms around her and keep her warm through the storm. But she was a princess, and he a lowly commoner. What would be the point in such fantasies?

He shook his head to clear it and then opened the door to head into the storm.

* * *

RAIN PELTED on Jayden's face. To call it a downpour would have been a vast understatement. Like much of what he'd seen these past few weeks, the storm had to be unnatural.

Lightning flashed, brightening the monastery's courtyard to give a brief glimpse of how bad the flooding had already become in the mere hours the storm had raged. The clouds darkened the entire sky, blotting the sun out as if it weren't even there. Even under the roof's overhang, Jayden couldn't help but get soaked to the core.

He regretted being too antsy to sit in the mess any longer. His clothes soaked through, bringing the chill to his skin and bones.

Another bolt flashed in the sky, but this time Jayden saw a figure standing in the courtyard. Did someone climb the hill during this torrential storm? They must have been exhausted, or at the very least, needed help.

"I see you!" Jayden shouted into the wind. His voice may have died across the courtyard. He had no way of knowing.

As the flash faded, it looked as if the figure stumbled. It would be difficult to get across the courtyard under these conditions.

Jayden muttered under his breath and made his way out of the safety of the overhang to help.

His eyes could hardly stay open. Each step became a battle against wind and rain as he pushed forward, hoping not to trip over the rocks, plants, or fountain in the area. He wished he'd had more layers of clothing or something to cover his head. Wishing wouldn't accomplish anything now. As much as the cold bothered him, it had to be far worse for this traveler.

Finally, he made it across the courtyard to where he'd seen the figure. Lightning flashed again, and it became clear in front of him, but Jayden found no weary traveler.

Bones stood before him, white, with nothing seeming to hold them together. A full skeleton hobbled in the rain—and it held a dagger in its hand. The skeleton swiped at Jayden's stomach.

Jayden sucked in his belly and jumped backward. The bones of the skeleton clattered as it moved, pressing forward, attacking Jayden. So much for a rescue attempt. Now, he had to face evil.

The skeleton came at Jayden with relentless pursuit. It swiped repeatedly with its blade, and Jayden could do little to defend himself. He didn't know how to hurt the skeleton, or even if he could do damage to it. How did one harm that which was already dead?

The rain and wind continued to beat down, and he slipped while he backed away from the evil creature. The slip saved him a knife flailing in the wind where he had stood, but it left Jayden in a disadvantageous position.

Jayden gripped a handful of mud and flung it at the skeleton. It seemed to confuse the creature. Even if it wouldn't do much to harm it, the act distracted the skeleton for a critical moment. Jayden scrambled to his feet and bolted away, backing toward the monastery.

His hand slipped on the doorknob, causing him to tense. The skeleton could be on his tail. On the second twist of the knob, the door opened. Jayden hurried inside and slammed the door behind him, breathing heavily.

Everyone gathered there turned their attention to him.

"Had enough of the rain?" Savrin asked.

Jayden's teeth chattered. "Skeleton…"

"That was foolish," Bronwyn said, standing and ushering him to a fire at the rear of the room. "I know it may sound improper, but you should remove your tunic and get yourself warm."

Jayden proceeded to the fire and stripped off his shirt without shame. Even years out of fighting shape, he had a muscular frame with very little fat on it. He rarely had the coin to afford extravagant meals, and carrying his instruments around often made his muscles sore.

Bronwyn's eyes descended over him. Jayden raised a brow at her. She blushed, but turned to find a blanket to throw over his shoulders. It brought him warmth, and soon he would dry. The monks brought him hot tea to warm his insides as well.

"What were you saying about a skeleton?" Savrin asked.

"There's a skeleton out there," Jayden said, glancing back to the door. "I thought it was a wanderer caught in the rain trying to find shelter, but when I came close, I saw the creature for its true form. The skeleton had a dagger." It sounded absurd, but Savrin had experienced much the same recent events with spirits and other strange happenings. Those instances had become too frequent in too short a span to be mere coincidences.

Savrin frowned. "If it was after you, where did it go?"

In answer to his question, something smashed in the door. Wood splintered everywhere, and cold from the storm outside whipped into the large room. The fire flickered, hardly able to handle the wind.

In door stood not one skeleton, but *six*. They crowded each other, pushing through the small space as if having no mind but for their target.

"There they are!" Jayden said.

Lord Hardwick drew a sword. "This is a bad omen indeed."

"Omen?" Savrin asked. "It's a current danger." He flashed his dagger into his hand.

As the skeletons approached, the monks muttered prayers, readying their staves for combat.

The fighting began, a deadly clash as one monk fell to a skeletal blow within moments. The others met with the undead counterparts, holding their own.

Savrin struck like the wind, hitting the skeletons several times with his blade. As Jayden had worried, the attack had little effect. Savrin's daggers could cut through bone, but the skeleton remained intact.

"This isn't working," Savrin said.

Menek dropped back behind the other monks and prayed again. Whether the prayer would work or not, Jayden couldn't be sure, but they had to clear an escape path if they aimed to survive the encounter. Hopefully, no more of those wicked creatures lay beyond the door.

Jayden kicked one skeleton, staggering it and forcing it away from him. "Come," he said, using the opening to make a run for it.

A couple of the monks followed, but two more stayed to guard Menek as he prayed.

Now on the opposite side of the skeletons, flanking them, Jayden wished the others would have followed his lead. This was no military unit at his command. His brothers would have seen the strategy he presented and followed without question.

Except Savrin, who maintained his flurry of a fight against the skeleton he had engaged.

But the skeletons didn't seem to care much about him or the monks. They had another purpose.

All of them moved toward Bronwyn, who stood frozen as a statue, trapped in the corner.

The skeleton which first reached her didn't stab at her, however. It grabbed her by the wrist. Another took her other arm. Bronwyn struggled and screamed, but she couldn't resist their force. They dragged her toward the door, not caring Jayden stood in their way.

Jayden intercepted them and attacked, but they fended him off with knives, shoving him aside to continue to the door.

As some skeletons disappeared out of the door, Menek finished his prayer. His eyes opened and appeared consumed with fire. He exhaled, and as he did so, he breathed out flame toward one of the closest skeletons. The flame incinerated its bones, and it collapsed into ash in front of them.

The sight made several of the other monks gawk, seemingly as unaware of this tremendous power as Jayden was. In that moment of distraction, the skeletons carrying Bronwyn made it to the door.

Menek and his monks rushed the horde of remaining skeletons, but one jammed the door to provide a shield for the others' escape. Bronwyn kept screaming, the sound of her voice trailing and fading into the storm outside.

The monk blew another breath of fire, disintegrating the skeleton at the door. Jayden rushed out, but it was too late. Bronwyn was gone. He staggered back inside, mentally checking off what needed to be done.

Lord Hardwick's face had gone pale. As much as he spoke of the business of prophecy, the sight of strange wonders had him in shock. Savrin patted him on the back to jolt him out of it. "Interesting times we live in," Savrin said.

"You can say that again," breathed Harwick. "What do we do now?"

"We rescue the princess," Jayden said. It was his duty, even if he could consider himself a soldier no longer. He vowed not to let these creatures hurt Bronwyn. "Is there a weapons cache here?"

"In the store room," one monk said.

"Someone get me a sword," Jayden said.

* * *

JAYDEN TRAVERSED outside into the storm, accompanied by several monks. This time, he came prepared. The monks outfitted him with a cloak to cover his head, and they had found him the sword he had asked for. What good would a sword do against the skeletons? So far, normal weapons had little effect, but the steel in his hands gave him a sense of strength—a measure of safety. It would be harder for the infernal creatures to stab him with their daggers, at the very least.

The monks' true weapon would be Menek, who taught several of his companions the prayer he used to summon the flames. Not all the monks were capable of it. It had something to do with the strength of their faith, or at least so Menek claimed. Jarrod mastered the prayer in no time, giving them at least two monks with the capability.

The group had agreed Lord Hardwick would stay behind with a protectorate of two monks. His knowledge might be necessary in the days to come if Jayden and the others failed.

The party set forward into the storm. Jayden hoped the skeletons had not gone far, as it would be difficult to track them through this storm. With how it raged, the town below must be flooded, or worse. The poor residents had nothing they could do in these situations. This was the Holy City, however. Perhaps prayers would spare the faithful.

Once across the courtyard, Jayden could see the skeletons. They hadn't gone far at all. Six of them held onto Bronwyn. She lay flat in a pose that would have appeared to be floating on air if not for the hands of the skeletons holding her. They no longer gathered in an attack formation, but appeared preoccupied with the princess.

It gave Jayden and his companions an opening, but how could they effectively fight these things while they held onto Bronwyn? The monks couldn't send their flames toward them with her so close.

A great aura pulsed beyond the skeletons, enough to brighten the whole courtyard. It was like lightning, but emanating from the ground instead of the air. From the aura, a figure emerged—translucent and glowing in white. A face formed in the figure, but with holes where the eyes should be, they had empty sockets. The figure raised its hands over Bronwyn. Energy pulsed from it, and it seemed to draw something from the princess—what, Jayden could not tell.

Bronwyn writhed in pain.

Jayden could wait no longer to strike. The time figuring out a strategy to handle these vile beings was over. He rushed forward and struck at the skeletons. Two of them let go of Bronwyn during his assault, but the other four held her. Jayden used their distraction to draw them toward his party, and soon the two skeletons had separated from the aura.

"Now!" Jayden shouted.

Menek and Jarrod muttered their prayers and cast forth flame at the two skeletons.

Even in the rain and wind, the flame flew true at the undead bones. The heat scorched the bones, overcoming the elements. This prayer had to have been the most powerful force Jayden had ever encountered. If the Sorcerer King could harness this kind of power, he would be king of the world.

Jayden didn't want to go down the rabbit hole of those dark thoughts. He had to focus on the present. On Bronwyn.

The apparition spoke, its voice booming like thunder, yet in the tone of a snake's whisper. "Daughter of House Daya, long have I awaited one of your blood to travel to this place. I will secure atonement for your sins. For, as one fallen in service to Hyrum, I have never received what is due."

Savrin ran forward, holding his cross necklace up toward the spirit. "Be gone, devil! In the name of Jesus Christ!"

The figure turned to Savrin, opening its mouth wide. A wind blew from it, sending Savrin flying backward. He tumbled on the courtyard grounds.

"Savrin!" Jayden said. He wanted to rush to his friend's side, but Bronwyn's life hung in the balance. The rogue would survive. He pushed forward to reach the princess.

A bolt of lightning shot from the spirit's eyes, a warning shot to scorch the ground in front of Jayden. "No interference," the figure warned.

"What do you want with her?" Jayden cried. "Take my life instead of hers."

The spirit floated, the wind blowing it like a flag, held in place only by some unseen force. "Your line is not of House Daya. Your sacrifice will not be acceptable."

Jayden braved pushing forward again. He maneuvered around the skeletons to swipe his sword at the spirit. The sword cut through it, but did little except flail in the air.

The spirit ignored him, drawing more energy which pulsed toward Bronwyn. She howled from the pain as the treacherous force reached her.

Savrin's work with daggers failed. The monks fire-breathing waned as the rain came down harder and smothered the flames. Nothing they did had any effect. For the physical attacks, Jayden couldn't say he was surprised. But Savrin's faith-based warnings having no effect disconcerted him. How did this spirit differ from those they'd already encountered? At least this one could speak. It had a strength of presence the others he'd met had not.

The monks stood at the ready, but appeared just as dumbfounded as Jayden. What could the proper course here be?

"Please, spirit," Jayden plead. "Release her. If I am not a worthy sacrifice, what will it take?"

The spirit stopped drawing the energy from Bronwyn. She gasped for air. The spirit turned to face Jayden. "Recognition for our deeds. My men died for the line of Daya, and yet we are forgotten!"

This spirit seethed over some slight long ago. Jayden wasn't a historical scholar, so he knew little of the line of Daya—Bronwyn's ancestry—beyond her lineage being exceptional. Savrin didn't speak up, which meant he probably didn't know the details of her ancestry, either. But there was one who may have known. "Give me time, spirit. Your vengeance has waited for…" He couldn't be sure how long it had been since this spirit walked the physical realm. "…many years, yes? Will you give us time?"

The spirit floated in the wind silently for several moments. Then it spoke. "I will give you until the sun sets."

"May we bring the girl with us?" Savrin asked.

"No," the spirit said.

Jayden hadn't expected a positive answer. Being able to bargain at all was boon enough for now. It would be up to them to figure out how to quench the spirit's hatred and rescue Bronwyn.

* * *

THE TEAM RETREATED to the mess inside the monastery's walls, all soaked to the core. They gathered around the fire to warm themselves. Jayden recounted the events outside to Lord Hardwick, who would be Bronwyn's last hope.

"Do you know much about this line of Daya? What could the spirit have done which has been forgotten for these years? That it never received recognition for?"

Hardwick shook his head. "I'm uncertain. However, if we go back to Daya's time, perhaps historians will have recounted the great battles in one of our volumes. The spirit must be from here, in the Holy City, yes? In all these years, the royal line of Hyrum must have had no reason to visit this monastery. Princess Bronwyn's presence must have awakened something here."

"We have to find something soon. It's already dark outside from the storm. It'll be more difficult to handle these creatures at night," Jayden said.

"We'll get to work," Menek said. He directed his brethren to the books. Hardwick moved with him.

Time passed. Jayden dried again and finally lost the bite from the cold outside. He didn't want to go out again. He wanted to rest, but he had to protect Bronwyn if he could.

One of the monks raised a hand, bringing Hardwick over to him. He showed him a passage in one of the ancient tomes. Hardwick nodded several times.

"Looks positive," Savrin said.

"Let us hope," Jayden said.

Hardwick made his way back over to them. "I believe we found it. Daya was a queen in Hyrum five hundred years ago. At the time, the holy pontiff had not declared this church territory, but it was a city state ruled by one Lord Haganus the Terrible. Queen Daya led an assault here, but the walls were too difficult for her men to capture on their own. Because of it, she hired sea pirates who raided the city from the opposite side.

"The problem was, the men in her contingent assaulting the city weren't aware of the pirates working for them as mercenaries. The pirates were slaughtered when the invasion force broke through on the other side, after doing much work to weaken Lord Haganus's line. Hyrum's army seized the city and slaughtered the pirates along with them. Queen Daya never mentioned them, as it didn't make for good publicity to note pirates had succeeded and made it easy for her armies, and so they became lost to history."

"How do you know about it?" Savrin asked.

"Our order takes copious notes always," Menek said proudly. "We are beholden to no monarch."

"Did the pirates have a name?" Jayden asked.

Jarrod nodded. "The Cool Wreath Pirates."

Savrin put up his hands in frustration. "What good does this do us? The pirates were slaughtered and they want revenge. Calling on the name of Christ does nothing to the spirit—the soul must have been a believer. We're stuck at square one, but now we know the spirit's cause is somewhat justified."

Jayden paced back and forth a few times as he thought about what the spirit had said. It was looking for recognition. Nothing more, nothing less. Bronwyn couldn't provide it because she had no idea about this ancient history. It would be difficult to satisfy this spirit, perhaps impossible to give it the respect due for winning a siege.

But there was one thing he could try.

"I have an idea," Jayden said. "I pray it's enough."

* * *

JAYDEN EXITED the storage room nearly an hour later. It would be sunset soon, and he hoped he still had the time. The monks carried a large case forward, trailing behind Jayden as he paced confidently toward the apparition and its gang of skeletons.

The spirit waited, rain and wind still beating down as hard as ever. Bronwyn lay limp and unconscious, held up by the skeletal beings.

When everyone was present, Jayden stepped forward.

"O, spirit representing the Cool Wreath Pirates. I come to do you honor, to remember your sacrifice in the best way I can. If you would calm the elements in this area?"

The spirit peered at him for a long moment. Then, a bubble of calm weather formed around the party. No rain entered within its bounds, as if some shell of energy came from the spirit, protecting them.

"I am listening," the spirit said.

Jayden nodded to Menek, who opened the case and brought forth his harp and handed it to him.

"I have written you a song, as is my task as a bard in service to Princess Bronwyn of Hyrum, daughter of the line of Daya. Please accept this gift." Jayden rested his fingers on the strings, taking a deep breath. He hadn't had nearly enough time to practice, and his fingers were wet from the small sojourn into the courtyard, but it would have to do.

He played a melody, somber at first, but then it crescendoed into a bright chorus which exemplified the pirates' victories. Along with it, he sang:

> *Long ago and far away, as songs of honor tell*
> *The Pirates of the Cool Wreath fought skillfully and well.*
> *When Queen Daya first asked them to help her save her land*
> *The Pirates of the Cool Wreath were there at her command*

> *While armies breached the east side, the pirates breached the West*
> *They brought the city to its knees, as each man did his best*
> *Her armies never heard of what Queen Daya did plan*

*And the Pirates of the Cool Wreath were slaughtered to a man.*


*And when the Queen discovered the wrong that she had done*
*She never told their families, their friends or anyone*
*Their graves along the seashore forgotten they now lie*
*And all their wives and children in sorrow they did cry.*


*Today we right a wrong and reveal their story sad*
*For where the Queen was noble, her strategy was bad.*
*We do not hide their story, nor shelter such a wrong*
*We celebrate the pirates, both in story and in song.*


His eyes closed as envisioned the age past through his song. The seamen coming ashore, raiding the city, slaughtering the guards and making it ripe for invasion from the Hyrum forces. It was better to get into the moment, forget where his fingers hit the strings—not thinking, and giving into the emotion of the song. The performance made his soul swell with pride. This was his calling.

When he finished, he opened his eyes again to see the spirit in front of him.

Another moment passed, and the spirit whirred into a funnel of air. It cried, but with tears of joy. Rain water flew from it as it glowed and raised into the heavens above.

The skeletons lost their cohesion and shattered beneath Bronwyn. Savrin rushed ahead to catch her before she fell.

Jayden handed the harp back to the monks, who carefully placed it in its case.

Once the spirit was gone, the sky cleared. The clouds shimmered away into the early evening sky, pinks, oranges, and reds filling the horizon. The city streets below had flooded, reflecting the light upward. Everything glowed with a heavenly serenity.

Menek placed his hand on Jayden's shoulder. "Your song could stir the Seraphim themselves. Come. Let's get warm once more for the evening and rest. You must try our brew."

"I would be happy to," Jayden said with a sigh of relief.

The party returned to the mess for the final time, Savrin carrying Bronwyn the whole way. The danger had ended. For now.

5

—————

OVER THE NEXT SEVERAL DAYS, JAYDEN HELPED THE MONKS CARE FOR the Holy City. The flood damage had left many people without homes —and with spoiled food. The monastery, being up on a hill, didn't suffer nearly as much as the areas below.

It didn't take long for the water to drain out to the sea, most of it receding into small creeks along the streets. Still, the people suffered.

The monks disbursed what goods they could to the citizens and used the strong backs of Jayden and Savrin for reconstruction efforts. Each day demanded hard work, followed by evening history lessons provided by Lord Hardwick.

Everyone agreed Jayden and Savrin should learn about the past, in order to better prepare them for the future.

One evening, they sat in the dining hall while Lord Hardwick quizzed Jayden on what he'd learned.

"When the ancients came to this world, what did they do?" Hardwick asked.

"They created the air and the seas in their first month, and then in their second, they brought the trees and plants. In the third month, they populated all the animals and the fish in the seas. Then, they set down in the Freelands and rested to enjoy the fruits of their labors, and there, the seeds of the Church Vigilant began," Jayden said.

"Very good," Hardwick said. "And what of the evil one?"

Savrin dropped back his mug of beer, leaving a frothy foam on his lips afterward. "The ancients sought a new Jerusalem, as per the Holy Bible's prophecy, but they could not remove sin from their flesh and bones. They thought in their hubris they would create a new heavenly kingdom, but instead retained the problems of the original fallen world. They brought with them a great evil, unleashing it upon the realm, and it brought about a hundred years of toil and torture before the ancient ones devised a way to imprison the Great Corrupter."

Hardwick nodded. "And where was the Corrupter imprisoned?"

"In The Demon's Eye Lake," Jayden said.

Menek and Jarrod stood behind Hardwick, watching as Savrin and Jayden answered the questions. They had their arms crossed, stoic in their countenance. "I believe our new friends have a good cursory knowledge of events," Menek said.

"I still don't understand what good this will do," Savrin said. "We have the harp relic. Aren't we supposed to do something with it?"

"We'll still have to research that matter," Hardwick said.

"And I must get more proficient at the instrument," Jayden said. He poured himself a fresh mug of beer.

"You've already done very well," Jarrod said. "I can see why you've been chosen by the Lord to deliver us from this dark period."

The words unsettled Jayden. He couldn't view himself as some prophesized savior. Savrin had only alluded to his being the chosen one, but these monks had already convinced themselves of it. He was a warrior-turned-musician. His eyes darted over toward Bronwyn, who sat by the fire alone, reading a tome on her lineage. She had been quiet ever since the rescue, and despite their awkward prior conversations, Jayden wished she would speak with him further.

She was so beautiful, and Jayden's eyes couldn't help but drift toward her ample bosom. His desires meant a failure in his character, Jayden understood. A lust for this woman. Further proof he couldn't be the one from the prophecies. How could the God of the Bible choose someone like him when he had such an impure heart? He sucked in his bottom lip with the thought.

"Don't worry too much," Menek said. "The burdens are hard, but the Lord will provide." He glanced to Jarrod and back again. "There is one matter we wished to discuss with you all the same."

"Oh?" Jayden asked.

"You believe in the One God, the Father Almighty, Maker of all the heavens and this earth, the one who brought the ancients here out of their desire to follow him, his one Son, who died and was buried, and on the third day rose again, and the Holy Ghost, who resides within us all as we wait for his return to usher us into the true heavenly kingdom."

The words didn't sound like a question, but Menek stared at Jayden as if waiting for an acknowledgement. In truth, Jayden hadn't considered these spiritual matters much before his odd quest with Savrin. He couldn't deny, however, the sights he had seen, the true evils in the world. If those existed, surely a counter to it did along with them, and, judging from the way the evils reacted to Savrin's cross, he had to admit the monks had something to their faith.

The people he'd met here had to be the most honest men he had ever encountered. One time, he would have thought such of his unit in Hyrum, but after seeing the behavior of all the soldiers save Savrin, he could no longer pretend his men had better morals than anyone else.

The group stared at him in earnest anticipation while Jayden deliberated. He had a feeling his answer would be an important moment in his life. "Yes, I believe," he said.

Those around him relaxed visibly, smiles breaking out amongst them. "Good," Menek said. "I want to offer you something. It's a ritual, a rite of passage one might say. It represents the cleansing of the soul and a commitment to the cause. You might think of it as a Lord bestowing knighthood on one of his men, but it is different."

Jarrod nodded. "It's called baptism. Have you heard of it?"

Jayden shook his head.

"We will douse you with holy water over your head," Menek said.

Some of the other monks brought a bowl of water to the table. "I cleansed the water and prayed over it earlier, in anticipation of this moment."

Jayden could tell this would be more than a mere ritual. A baptism would require him to commit himself to the cause of the Church Vigilant. If these signs and wonders continued, he may as well have the protection of God over him. "You may baptize me," Jayden said.

Savrin's eyes twinkled. Lord Hardwick, too, seemed pleased. Menek grabbed a towel, cupping his other hand in the bowl. He grabbed a handful of water and poured it over Jayden's head. "I baptize you in the name of the Father." He repeated the motion. "And of the Son." For a third time, he poured water over Jayden's head. "And of the Holy Ghost. Welcome, my brother, to the Church. We are blessed by your presence."

The monk wiped Jayden's forehead, and the entire group came forward to shake Jayden's hand and give him hugs. Joy filled Jayden, welling through his belly and up through his chest. Whether it came from his imagination or because the Holy Ghost filled him, he couldn't say. The baptism had been the right course of action, though. Jayden could feel it in his soul.

"Now what?" Jayden asked.

Before anyone could answer his question, a monk burst through the doors. "Brothers, we have intruders at the gates."

"More problems?" Savrin scoffed.

"A contingent of men brandishing swords," the monk said.

"Impossible. None but the approved monastic orders can carry weapons into the inner sanctum of the Holy City," Menek said. "Outsiders are met at the gates and told to leave their weapons aside."

"Possible or not, it's true," the monk said.

"You didn't check my weapons," Savrin said.

Jarrod shrugged. "You are one of us, even if you haven't taken our holy vows."

"You honor me," Savrin said.

Jayden shifted uncomfortably at the news. He wiped water, dripping down from his hair, from his brow. "I should protect the harp."

One of the other monks brought the harp case to him, ensuring it would be in his possession. Jayden clutched it.

Bronwyn stirred from her studies at the commotion, moving toward them. "Is something the matter?"

"We may have to defend ourselves, fair princess," Savrin said.

"Lord Hardwick and Lady Bronwyn must be protected," Menek said. "Perhaps we should hide them in the cellars?"

"I'll stand my ground with you, thank you," Lord Hardwick said defiantly.

"As will I," Bronwyn said, narrowing her eyes.

Jayden sighed. "You two will be the death of me. It's the job of soldiers to protect our valuable assets."

"Then we should be protecting you," Lord Hardwick said.

He couldn't argue with Hardwick's logic. If Jayden truly had to perform some song to complete prophecy and save this world, his life mattered more than the others'. He scrunched his nose at the thought. His entire life, he had been nobody of import. It didn't sit with him that God would choose him above others.

As they argued about who should protect who, the door swung open. Soldiers burst through, uniformed and armored, all with swords drawn. Their tabards and banners displayed the red and yellow colors of Hyrum. Behind them stood the Sorcerer King, cloaked in dark robes, his icy eyes landing on Jayden. "Seize him," the Sorcerer King said.

The soldiers moved to grab him, but the monks cut off their path. They formed an impenetrable line, and the tension of the situation gave the soldiers pause.

"Violence is not welcome in this sanctuary," Menek said.

"Spare me, priest," the Sorcerer King said. "You are harboring a fugitive of Hyrum—a very dangerous one. Give him to me, and return the princess whom he kidnapped, and we will leave your place in peace."

"They are my guests, and we will not cede them to you," Menek said, holding firm.

The Sorcerer King motioned his men forward.

The soldiers attacked. With their swords, they clashed with the monks and their staves. Hardwick foolishly joined the line of monks, trying to be a valiant hero. Jayden wanted to yell for him to retreat, but it would do no good. The man had a look of vengeance on his face, and no words would make him back down.

Lord Hardwick's blade met the steel of one soldier. By the way the Hyrum held formation, keeping with perfect sync and their sleek movements, Jayden could tell these weren't ordinary soldiers. The Sorcerer King had brought his elite guard.

The monks had no chance there.

"Cease the fighting!" Jayden said, but his words came too late.

One of the Hyrum soldiers parried Hardwick's blows, and in a counterassault, he ran his sword through Hardwick's belly.

Lord Hardwick lost his grip on his blade. He choked and then fell to his knees. Despite getting run through, he had a grin on his face. He raised his head skyward. "Lord, take me. I am ready to die in your service."

And then he collapsed the rest of the way.

The Hyrum soldier pulled his blade from Hardwick's body, ready to move on to the next.

The Sorcerer King bade his men hold back. "Does anyone else want to become a martyr? There is no one here to tell of your exploits in this."

"We will surrender," Jayden said.

The others looked at him as if he were mad.

"It's the only choice," he said, meeting Bronwyn's eyes. Her concern seemed so pure and innocent. Her thoughts mattered more to him than the others.

Blast it, he couldn't let his feelings dictate the situation, but he wouldn't have her die in some foolish skirmish they could not win.

The monks listened to him, the death of Lord Hardwick providing enough of a warning. They stepped aside to allow the soldiers access to Jayden.

Two soldiers grabbed him by the arms, another taking the harp. They also seized Bronwyn, Savrin, and Menek, disarming the two with weapons and pulling the monk along. As they bound the four, the Sorcerer King watched with his cool gaze.

Jayden could tell the Sorcerer King would not rest until he had his public execution. The brutal king cared more about his optics than anything else. An escaped prisoner was a matter he felt he had to deal with personally.

It made the situation all the more dangerous.

The guards ushered all of them out of the door, leaving the monks in stunned silence.

* * *

THE GUARDS JAMMED JAYDEN, Savrin, Bronwyn, and Menek inside a caged cart, the cage much too small to accommodate the four of them, and sealed the door. Bars ran lengthwise on all four sides. A soldier placed Jayden's harp next to the driver of the soldiers' carriage, so close, yet out of reach.

Jayden shifted uncomfortably to make more room for his broad shoulders. The driver whipped the horses' rears, and the cage moved. Another closed carriage followed behind them, presumably containing the Sorcerer King.

The guards walked on foot as the two carriages moved in a slow procession through the Holy City.

The streets made for a smooth ride, fortunately, because each time they went over a bump, it rattled the four of them in the cage. Savrin seemed to have the worst of it.

"What are we going to do?" Bronwyn asked, her lips close to Jayden's neck. He could feel her warm breath tickling his skin.

If only she breathed so close to him in a different situation.

Jayden grit his teeth and tried to focus. "I don't know," he said. From his position, he couldn't formulate a good plan.

The carriages moved slowly through the streets, attracting onlookers and bystanders. The people seemed confused, looking on at Jayden and his friends with scorn and derision before moving about their lives. It didn't bother Jayden, however. He didn't know any of these people, and likely would never see them again. Who cared if they thought him a lowly prisoner?

Menek muttered prayers, which he continued to do as they passed through the Holy City's gates, out to The King's Road, which led all the way to Hyrum and beyond.

Once on the open road, the ride became much less smooth, wheels catching on stones and in holes periodically, jostling the carriage and causing Jayden and the others to rattle and fall into one another. Jayden gripped the bars to keep himself steady, though his hands tired after the first hour.

Throughout the journey, Menek never ceased with his prayers.

Jayden found himself impressed with the monk's dedication. Though he was now baptized, he could never see himself being so dedicated as to pray without cease. His thoughts wandered too often, his ambitions remained too high.

Bronwyn shifted against him. Even with the clothes between them, she felt so soft, so warm. It could drive a man mad.

He had never thought of entertaining another love. Not until he'd met Bronwyn. How could this princess have replaced his dead lover so quickly? The thoughts unsettled him.

Jayden cursed under his breath.

"What's wrong?" Bronwyn asked.

"Nothing," Jayden said. He sounded terser than he meant to come off, but he couldn't find a good way to be firm with her and keep her from occupying his thoughts without the angry tone.

Her silence, no doubt driven by her thinking she had upset him, made matters worse.

Jayden let out a slow breath to remain calm. Stuck as he was in this God-forsaken cage, he couldn't do much but brood. Other than pray like Menek, he supposed.

He closed his eyes. *God, get me out of this.*

Simple, but it was all he could think to pray. He couldn't be so verbose as the monks or the others he heard. How did they utter so many words all the time?

The carriage went over another hole in the road, bouncing them in the cage. The jolt made Jayden lose his balance, even while holding onto the bars. He smooshed back into Bronwyn, who leaned on the others, shifting the weight of the entire cage. As he righted himself, he turned.

The cage door popped open.

"We're free!" Savrin said under his breath, not wanting to alert the guards on the side of the road. "We're going to have to make a move for it quickly."

Jayden took in their surroundings. "The forest to the right looks thick. We should head there."

"All together," Menek agreed. "One… Two…"

The monk hurried out the back, bolting for the forested area. Savrin kept right on his heels, the rogue always quick to move. Bronwyn hesitated, but tiptoed out of the carriage and ran after them, leaving Jayden to bring up the rear.

Jayden turned, keeping pace with the carriage. The guards in the following carriage hadn't noticed their escape yet, nor had the walking guards. He had to get his harp before joining the others. It wouldn't be too far. Perhaps he could sneak out before anyone noticed.

"Prisoner escape!" A soldier shouted.

So much for that idea.

Jayden hurried to the harp, grabbing the case and flinging it wildly around to prevent any soldiers from getting too close to him. Several of them lost pace with the carriage from his maneuver, falling behind to the second carriage containing the Sorcerer King and his entourage.

The harp weighed him down, and slowed his pace. The others had already reached the tree line. Fortunately, the Sorcerer King had given no orders to kill them. The archers wouldn't fire. Their escape would depend on fooling the swordsmen and outmaneuvering them.

Ready for the task, Jayden took off running as hard as he could to the forest, keeping the clunky harp within his hands. His arms burned as much as his legs during the run, his whole body engaged. Worse, his lungs took the most toll. He couldn't move as fast as he had when he was a youth in the Sorcerer King's army. Those days seemed ages ago.

The guards followed, hot on his tail, calling out to others to give chase. Jayden didn't dare look back. It would slow his pace, something he couldn't afford. Plus, he couldn't lose his friends as the trees thickened into a darker region of the forest.

Jayden kept pace with his friends, even while holding the harp. Savrin led the pack, weaving between trees with an expertise and ease Jayden envied. His maneuvering threw some soldiers off their trail as they continued into the forest. Soon, it appeared as if they would be in the clear, as the soldiers backed away to return to their leader. They'd ventured far enough to evade the Sorcerer King's men.

Savrin slowed his pace, as did the others, giving everyone a chance to catch their breaths.

Menek, out of all four of them, didn't even breathe heavily.

"Light run?" Savrin asked.

Menek shrugged. "Nothing compared to standing on one hand for an hour, your head perilously close to hot coals, attempting to maintain meditation and concentration on the Lord God."

"Sounds delightful," Savrin said, shaking his head. "We shouldn't linger here for too long."

'Haven't we lost them?" Bronwyn asked.

"A good question," came a deep and booming voice from behind them. The voice of the Sorcerer King.

They hadn't lost the soldiers at all. His guards arrived with him. Others came from the trees opposite. Their pursuers had gone to flank them and give them a false sense of security. They had fallen for a basic trap.

Jayden cursed himself under his breath. He should have known better. So should have Savrin.

Bronwyn only gazed at him in a distant hope he would have a new plan.

* * *

SAVRIN CHARGED FORWARD, waving his dagger in the air.

Jayden winced, holding the harp case while watching his friend make a rash move. He understood Savrin's motivations. It would be better to go in battle than be dragged off and executed in some public display. But by the same token, they'd had one chance to escape. There might be another.

The soldiers grabbed Savrin by the arms as he swung his dagger. He drove the point into armor, the metal clanging against it. The soldier twisted Savrin's arm to force him to drop the weapon. Soon, they had him restrained, with another soldier bringing rope to tie his hands behind his back.

Savrin bucked like a wild bull, but he only futilely expended his energy. The soldiers took no pity on him, dropping him to the ground and pressing his face against the dirt with their boots. The fire dimmed from his eyes as he realized he'd ushered in his own defeat, and soon he stopped moving.

"Does anyone else want to make a fruitless display?" the Sorcerer King asked.

No one spoke. Jayden stared at the monarch, meeting his eyes defiantly as few had ever done.

The Sorcerer King approached Jayden, confidence in his dark eyes —and anger. His lips twitched. He stopped directly in front of Jayden's face. "You've caused me all sorts of problems since I found you. My diviners say your destiny is to cause even more."

Jayden kept his face stoic, not wanting to show any sign of weakness.

"Perhaps instead of making a public display of your execution, I should end your life here and be done with it. It would be the most prudent course of action." He noticed the case in Jayden's hands, pressing his finger hard against it. "What's in here?"

"Nothing that will matter to you," Jayden said.

"Open it," the Sorcerer King demanded.

Jayden enjoyed rebelling, but it wouldn't be a good idea to deny his every request. He didn't want to encourage his wrath and get the Sorcerer King to reconsider killing him on the spot. He set the case on one point, releasing the clips and opening it to reveal the ancient harp in all of its glory.

The Sorcerer King laughed. "A harp? I admit, I know little about you, deserter, but I expected to find some magical, infernal device. This is all you have? My nemesis is attempting to become a bard?" His laughing continued as he spun on his heels and walked away from Jayden. Some of the soldiers chuckled along with him, clearly trying to please their Lord.

Then, the Sorcerer King turned around again. "Well, bard, play for us! Perhaps your music will be worth your life and you can become a servant in my courts." His eyes glinted, mocking.

The soldiers grinned and mocked Jayden, but he held still.

Menek leaned close to whisper into his ear. "Play as he says. A lullaby."

Jayden wanted to ask why he should do anything the Sorcerer King demanded, especially with the derision the soldiers thrust upon him, but when the monk spoke, he bestowed truths. He should comply. He searched his mind for a song which would qualify as a lullaby, recalling one he'd heard when he was young.

All eyes descended on him. The forest quieted.

Jayden took the harp into his hand. He hit one note, humming another as he recalled the song in its entirety. It had been such a long time.

From behind him, Menek offered a prayer to God.

"Well? We don't want to wait here all night," the Sorcerer King said.

Jayden breathed, trying to relax in the bizarre situation. The soldiers had grins on their faces he wanted to wipe off with a good fist to their jaws, but he would play. It was what he had wanted to do, hadn't it been? To play for kings, to be known for something other than the prowess of his sword—his artistic creation.

His fingers danced along the strings of the harp, playing a slow and mellow tune, falling into a rhythmic pattern he remembered. The song was one about being carried away on a gryphon to a magical land with lots of colors. He sang the lyrics as he recalled them:

*Through my window one night, when I once was a child*
*A gryphon flew singing, his tones low and mild*
*I'll show you such wonders you've never known*
*You'll remember these rainbows still when you have grown.*


*Through my window I climbed, and we flew through the sky*
*The rainbows flew round me and never asked why*
*For my sorrow they saw, and the pain set apart,*
*Yet the Song of the Gryphon still soothes my young heart,*


*Sleep soft, my sweet child, let me sing you a song*
*It's safe now to sleep while we travel along*
*The rainbows will guard you wherever you are*
*And the angel who guides you looks down from the stars.*

HIS EYES CLOSED, envisioning the world from the song—a place with no darkness, no war, no horrors or death, only magical creatures who comforted him. Laughter and joy dwelled in that world, one he may never see, or perhaps it would be one he would visit soon enough when the Sorcerer King decided he tired of Jayden's playing. He had escaped his doom two times already, more than any man ought to count upon. He should consider himself lucky for the extra time he'd gained.

This performance would be the swan song of his life. But he didn't fret about it, instead he let the music play itself, and focused on the feeling. It filled him with peace, despite the circumstances. Part of him wanted to fall asleep with his mother singing the tune, tucking him into his bed. Those days seemed so long ago.

Soon enough, the song ended. Jayden let his hands fall from the harp, and he took in a long breath before reopening his eyes.

When his sight acclimated to the dark forest, what he saw astounded him.

All the soldiers had fallen asleep, as had the Sorcerer King and Bronwyn. Only he, Menek, and Savrin remained awake.

"I don't know what you did, but praise the Lord," Savrin said.

"Truly," Menek said, grinning.

Jayden hurried his harp back into his case, clasping it before picking it up again. "Savrin, can you stir the princess?"

Savrin leaned over and shook Bronwyn several times. She awoke slowly, looking hazy eyed as she did so. "What happened? Are we dead?"

"Not if we move quickly," Jayden said.

"Menek said a prayer," Savrin said. "It filled the harp with some holy spell which put everyone to sleep."

"Why did we stay awake?" Jayden asked, glancing at the monk.

Menek shrugged. "The Lord works in mysterious ways. But we have more important questions to posit. Where will go?"

"Easy," Jayden said, securing the harp and starting south. "We'll go over the border into Tyril. We'll be safe there." *At least for a time. Until the country is invaded*, he thought.

The party hurried from the scene, but said no more until they were far out of earshot of the soldiers, as to not stir their enemies.

6

THE PATRONS AT THE EMPTY DRAUGHT INN WERE FREE WITH THEIR libations and with their tips.

It kept Jayden playing for three nights straight. He could get used to working the music scene here. The Innkeeper asked him if he wanted to come on full time, but something in him told him he would be on the move soon enough, and he wouldn't be able to commit to such a task.

It marked the first time anyone cared about his music or seemed to take an interest in his talent. Could the ancients' harp have that much of an impact on his skill? It provided him with confidence, something he'd lacked before. He'd felt like a mediocre musician at best. Now, he sounded like a master. It helped that the harp had more of a dynamic range than a gittern, with notes that could overlap and ring out for a long time. It covered the mistakes.

But his singing had gotten better too. The women in the inn took more notice of him. Returning their smiles didn't make Bronwyn very happy. Fortunately, no one recognized the princess. She'd been out of sight for so long in Hyrum, it was no wonder the Tyril people didn't remember her appearance.

He finished up the night's set, receiving a mug of beer from the innkeeper to quench his thirst, when Savrin came through the door.

"Look what the cat dragged in," Jayden said.

The rogue had been gone since they had arrived in Rosenton, a town about two days' journey from the border. They didn't want to stop at one of the border towns proper, in case the Sorcerer King brought his armies into the town to seize them. After a time, Jayden determined the party had traveled far enough away to where they'd be able to rest. Though, in truth, it was now about time they moved on, before someone reported their whereabouts.

What Savrin had been up to in the meantime, Jayden had no idea.

"Where have you been?" Jayden asked.

"I'll have you know, I did a fair amount of reconnaissance work the last three days while you were playing around." He made a little motion mocking Jayden's harp-playing movements. "It wasn't easy, either. No living in a cozy inn room. I had to sleep in the forest."

"Poor you," Jayden said.

"Damn right," Savrin nodded. He harrumphed and ordered a glass of ale from the innkeeper. "Anyway, the Sorcerer King has been quiet. I would have expected him to be livid and send his full army after us, knowing his penchant for vengeance."

"If he made a scene, it would embarrass him," Jayden said.

"That it would."

"He doesn't like being embarrassed." Jayden recalled how angry the Sorcerer King had been in the palace.

"You figured that out? I'm surprised they didn't hunt us down when we left the service the first time," Savrin said.

"What did you learn?" Jayden asked.

The ale arrived. Savrin took the cup into his hand, dropping it back in a big gulp before burping and setting the cup down. Foam fizzled on his upper lip. "He's gathering his armies, but it doesn't look like he's coming after us. There must be something more important he's doing. Which is disconcerting. He may have learned something from the monks, if he had one interrogated. We should assume he knows of the prophecies and your involvement in them. He will probably seize these evil powers bubbling up from the earth for his own ambitions."

"Sounds delightful," Bronwyn said, leaning against the bar near Jayden. "May I have a drink, too?"

Jayden raised his hand to flag the innkeeper down and get a cup for Bronwyn. When she received her drink, the three of them clanked their mugs together. "To friendship. Hopefully it won't be a short one."

"Indeed. Though we do have a new mission, one which could prove dangerous," Savrin said.

"Again?" Jayden asked.

"Don't give me that skeptical look. Last time I brought you on a quest, you walked away with that harp." Savrin motioned to Jayden's instrument.

"That I did," Jayden said, glancing at the harp. It glimmered in the soft light of the fire. He was glad he found it, and now he wouldn't want to perform without the instrument. Savrin had come through. "Where will we be going, then?"

"The Deadlands."

Bronwyn gasped. "It's dangerous there! You're mad."

"Not mad. Before he died, Lord Hardwick analyzed texts pertaining to the ancients and their imprisonment of the demon, and learned they likely began their work there. After talking to our monk friends, they told me there may be old scrolls to help us ensure the evil doesn't fully enter this world."

"I hope it's not too late," Jayden said.

"I'll make preparations to go, then," Bronwyn said.

Jayden shook his head. "Why don't you stay here? My tips can fund you staying in this inn for at least a fortnight. As you said, the place is dangerous."

Bronwyn crossed her arms over her chest. Unfortunately, it made Jayden's eyes focus there, and she glowered at him. "I am not staying behind. I know nothing about these prophecies, but I have no place to go until the Sorcerer King is dethroned."

"I'll leave you two to sort it out, while I go find Menek," Savrin said, scooping up his mug and finally removing the foam from this upper lip.

"He'll be in room three, praying," Jayden called as the rogue left them. Menek wouldn't join them for libations in the inn. Though the monks made their own ale, he didn't want to partake in the secular place. Jayden didn't understand. He enjoyed playing music for people willing to listen and loved the feeling of being around so many having a good time.

"You're not going to leave me here," Bronwyn said.

Jayden sighed. "We can't have a woman slowing us down on these quests. The monks can protect you as well as we can. Don't you think you're too important to be gallivanting across the continent?"

"No more important than you. You're the one who has to handle this prophecy, or whatever it is." Bronwyn waved flippantly. "Besides, I trust you. You won't let harm come to me." Her eyes darted away from him. What did she mean by all of this?

"I do what I must," Jayden said. He wanted to say more, to get to know her better somehow.

"So do I. I won't stay." Her eyes met his again.

She was so beautiful. He wanted nothing more in that moment but to kiss her. His one taste of her lips only left him hungry for more. But he shouldn't. He had to solve the wrongs of the world. People were counting on him, whether they knew it or not. He'd seen the spirits of the dead. Things had to return to normalcy before he could think of base passions.

* * *

With the help of the monks, they rented a cart and horses, promising to return them in three weeks' time. Menek manned the horses up front, while Jayden, Savrin, and Bronwyn sat in the back of the cart. The bumps in the road on the way out of Tyril reminded him of being trapped in the Sorcerer King's cage. It jostled them around similarly, though with more space and less to worry about.

Heading to the frontier of the Deadlands meant the road wouldn't be as well-maintained as the one between Tyril and Hyrum. Merchants didn't frequent the Deadlands, where abominations and other strange creatures prowled its plains and the desert beyond. Some barbarian tribes roamed the lands, making it possible to do trade, but the risk far outweighed the rewards.

They continued along the road, quiet most of the way, until Savrin broke the silence. "I think I'm going to move up front."

"Why?" both Bronwyn and Jayden asked at the same time.

"Because the tension back here is enough to drive a man mad. The two of you could probably use some time alone." Without waiting for a reply, he turned to the front of the cart where Menek sat, hopping over the railing.

Bronwyn flushed a bright red. Something about her cheeks becoming rosier made her irresistible to Jayden. Her innocence, her beauty—it struck him like a bludgeon to the gut, giving him twisting butterflies.

It took everything in him not to reach across the cart, grab her, and force her into a passionate kiss. She probably would have been receptive to it, given her shy glances. But they remained as quiet as before. Neither of them moved. What could they do or say? Now wouldn't be the time to form such a relationship, even if they wanted to. Moreover, she would probably have a number of more respectable suitors, once she returned to claim her throne. Jayden could never deserve her.

"I'm sorry to make the journey awkward," Bronwyn said quietly, breaking the silence.

"There is no problem with you, Princess," Jayden said. "Other than I still believe it's too dangerous for you to be here."

Bronwyn pushed a strand of blonde hair back behind her ear. "I appreciate your protectiveness. Your loyalty has so far proved to be greater even than my house guards..." She trailed off, eyes darting to the distance, longing and sad.

"They abandoned you for the Sorcerer King?" Jayden asked. His fists clenched at the thought. The disloyalty of men to appease those in power upset him to his core. Perhaps there were those who would call him disloyal for abandoning his post, but he stayed true to his principles at all costs. And he would stay true to Bronwyn, relationship or no. She deserved his care and respect.

Bronwyn nodded. "People I had known since birth."

"That must be hard," Jayden said. He sympathized. He'd had a bond with his unit like family. When they couldn't see the atrocities they committed in the name of a tyrant, and turned their backs on him, it had crushed his spirit for a long time. He fell into a dark place, where he could barely function for months. He'd done a lot of drinking then, but finally came out the other side with a passion for music. It filled the void to some extent, but he still missed the camaraderie. At least he still had Savrin, though he wouldn't tell the rogue how much he meant to him.

"It is," Bronwyn said, frowning. "I want things to go back to the way they were, with father and mother and sister and brother, before the Sorcerer King snaked his way into power as an advisor. Why didn't anyone seen his ambitions then? We were all so taken with his magicks..."

"Such is the way of devilry," Jayden said. "It sneaks in under the guise of something helpful. Once it has you in its clutches is the only time it shows its true, ugly head. At least you won't be so quick to trust those using unholy magicks in the future."

"You're so calm about everything, like there's a life lesson to be learned."

"There is."

"I know, but shouldn't good and right be the ones to win? It's not fair," Bronwyn said.

"It's not, but I can't do anything about it, so I'll only fret about what I can control." Jayden reached a hand across the cart toward her. He was not trying to chastise her or lecture her, and hoped it was apparent.

Bronwyn looked down at his hand and then reached to take it. Her skin was soft and cool, though the touch warmed Jayden nonetheless. His fingers slipped into hers, entwining. Their eyes locked, and though his first impulse was to turn aside, he maintained his gaze. She relied on his strength. It would be best to show it.

"Thank you," Bronwyn said.

"Of course," Jayden said.

Savrin glanced back, his eyes twinkling, a big grin on his face. He didn't say anything to ruin the moment—thank the Lord.

Jayden wanted a genuine connection with Bronwyn, but he also didn't want to get too close to her. Though by the same token, he couldn't recall when he'd had such a good conversation with a woman. He'd finally attained something with her, something he couldn't define just yet, and he didn't want to let it go.

The sun set over the horizon, turning the sky pink and red. Small dunes littered the horizon.

Menek pulled the cart to the side of the road, aiming for a flat clearing on the plains, where few plants grew. "This looks like a good place to make camp. We can see all around us, and we can set up tents early so we can have a good fire and meal."

"Sounds good by me," Savrin said. "I'm starving."

The moment passed, and Jayden released Bronwyn's hand to unload the cart. It hurt, prying himself from her. But she would still be there with him, wouldn't she?

* * *

MENEK HAD BUILT a sturdy fire at their encampment. The flames waved toward the east, the direction they would travel in the morning. Jayden clutched his cup of tea, the steam rising and warming his face. He sat on a log he'd found and moved over toward the fire. His watch would end soon, and he'd wake Savrin and get himself a few more hours sleep.

Jayden yawned. Despite the tea, he could hardly keep himself awake anymore. He blinked several times, wishing he had Bronwyn or even one of the others to talk to.

It was better she slept soundly away from him. The temptations to wake her and steal kisses from her ran through his head, but he had to keep their relationship in check until they could get into a more stable situation. It wouldn't be fair to her otherwise. He hated thinking about her over and over like he had been doing, but he couldn't control it. She had a grip on his heart like no other had in recent memory.

None since Huldra.

His chest constricted with a pain he'd thought long gone. He'd tried to forget Huldra as best he could. She would never come back. It was part of why he didn't want to move too quickly with Bronwyn. The excuses of "it's for her sake" were convenient, but it came back to not wanting to lose someone again.

Jayden sighed, finally admitting it to himself. He loved Bronwyn.

Something rustled outside the camp, pulling him from his thoughts.

Darkness covered everything beyond the camp. It was a new moon, with less light than usual. He couldn't see anything.

Jayden gripped the sword he had lying beside his seat. He'd had to grip steel much more often than he cared for as of late, but with the way fate pushed him, it had become unavoidable. Grunting, he pushed himself up to stand.

No sound came from the darkness ahead, but Jayden narrowed his eyes to peer, anyway. It was useless. He could see nothing in this light. He would have to leave the fire and let his eyes adjust to get a clearer picture of whatever lurked out there.

The rustling sound came again. This time, shadows moved in the darkness. They had the shape of men, not animals. Bandits.

Jayden turned, hurrying into the tents. Savrin slept soundly, but Jayden prodded him with his boot. "Savrin. We have company."

The rogue stirred, eyes glazed over at first, until the situation struck him. He popped out of his blankets, scrambling to get his boots on. "How many are there?"

"I couldn't get a good look," Jayden said, then prodded Menek with his boot.

The monk stirred to alertness. He could hear Bronwyn stirring in her tent as well. Jayden took lead and made his way out of the front of the tent.

The invaders had already arrived, more than a dozen of them.

To Jaden's surprise, no men stood before him.

Standing at seven feet in height, and wider than a human, these creatures had short arms, scales, and eyes as black as the night beyond. Giant teeth protruded from their mouths, giving them wicked grins on their faces. One snap of their jaws would be deadly.

Some had swords, others had spears, and the sharp tips pointed directly at Jayden and his friends.

There would be no way to overcome these monsters.

"The Lizard people," Menek said under his breath. "Notorious packs of them roam the Deadlands. It's impossible to reason with them."

Jayden hadn't heard of Lizard people before, but the words described these creatures well. None trembled at their ugly visages, not even Bronwyn. They had grown accustomed to strange sights. This was the reason civilized men didn't venture this far east, other than taking ships over to the Freelands.

One lizard, with a thick silver chain around its neck, hissed. The others followed with similar sounds, a wash of noise overcoming the encampment. This had to be their language, but Jayden couldn't understand.

"We surrender," Jayden said, setting his sword at his feet to demonstrate his sincerity. He held his hands up.

The lead Lizard pointed to him, and others grabbed Jayden, pulling him forward. Another made a motion which appeared to demand the others do the same.

Following Jayden's lead, the party dropped their weapons. The Lizards took them away from the encampment, leaving all the humans' possessions behind. These weren't bandits—they had to want them for some other purpose.

* * *

AFTER AN HOUR'S WALK, the Lizard people led them to a small city built of large stones. Instead of doors and regular houses, the Lizard people burrowed under the stones, leaving small entrances to slither inside. The raiding group led Jayden to one such opening. They prodded Jayden with a spear to get him to move, pushing him onto his belly to crawl under the opening.

When he made his way through, it opened into a large cavern beneath the rock, hollowed out, with torches lighting it, much like the halls of any great lord in Hyrum or Tyril, but well underground. The large room had several other Lizards inside, all with spears, and one clinging to a wall behind the dais, right by two heavy burning torches, basking in the light and heat.

The room had expert engineering. The smoke from the torches billowed into chutes above them, rising out of the place, while other such holes above allowed fresh air inside.

The Lizard on the wall had a sand coloration to it, while the others appeared green. The skin tone must have signified status.

"These are the hew-mons tresssssspasssssssing our landsssss," the creature on the wall said in a whispery hiss. At least it spoke the common King's language.

"We are passing through on a holy quest in the name of our Lord Jesus Christ," Menek said, stepping up from behind Jayden. "We do not mean to intrude on your domain."

The Lizards shifted uncomfortably at the invocation of the name of God. They shivered collectively, the shaking causing a rustling in the room.

"You will not utter that name again," the sand-colored Lizard said. "We are in need of a sssssacrifice to our goddesssss. Take them to the pit." The sand-colored Lizard scurried up the wall, behind a small rock face, out of sight.

The guards prodded them again, pushing them back toward the entrance. Bronwyn stayed close to Jayden, visibly shaken, her eyes wide with fear. She clutched Jayden's arm, digging her nails into it.

Even though the tight grip hurt, Jayden said nothing. He had to remain strong for her, to keep her calm. This pit didn't sound inviting.

Once out of the underground room, the Lizards led them deeper into their town. In the middle of it was a large open circle, which at first Jayden thought was a gathering place, until he saw the cliff in front of him, leading into darkness below.

Dozens of Lizards gathered there before five fires surrounding the pit. Some Lizards played a feral rhythm on drums, while others chanted in their strange hissing language. Robe-clad Lizards, with their heads covered, bowed before the pit, their tails erect behind them.

They had entered some strange religious ritual. Though he couldn't see anything, a spiritual presence made itself known before Jayden—heavy, angry, evil. A devil masquerading as a goddess had deceived these creatures.

But what could he do to stop it? So far, the invocation of Christ or his harp playing had stopped but he didn't have his harp with him. The cross dangled from Savrin's neck, but it didn't create a strong enough effect. Menek said prayers as he usually did: calm, steady, and regular.

Lizards circled them, dancing in a strange rhythm and spraying them from perforated cups with a foul-smelling substance.

"What are they going to do with us?" Bronwyn asked.

A procession came forward, carrying torches, and in between them, six more Lizards held a large flank of some rank meat, dripping with blood as they came through. Poles supported the meat, stabbing through it and swaying with each step the Lizards took. They stepped to the edge of the pit and held the meat out over it.

The earth rumbled. Jayden struggled to keep his footing. Bronwyn held onto him.

From the pit came a giant worm creature, barely able to fit within its opening. It reared its head, opening a giant maw with rotting, pointed teeth. The creature then snapped its jaw shut around the meat, and lowered itself again, tugging the meat off of the pole. When it came to rest, its mouth lingered barely a foot below the opening.

The Lizards cheered and chanted. The drums beat louder.

Sweat dripped down Jayden's brow. He didn't see a way out of this one. It became clear the Lizards intended to feed them to this creature in some sacrifice to a profane goddess.

Menek placed a hand on Jayden's shoulder. "Fear not. The Lord will protect us," he said.

"I don't feel very protected right now," Savrin said. The rogue losing his witty banter only made the situation more frightening. Savrin never showed fear.

A spear prodded Jayden, forcing him forward toward the cliff. He dragged his feet closer and closer to the edge, the others with him. Bronwyn took his hand and held it tightly. The spears prodded at them again.

The great maw opened below. Jayden's foot slipped on the edge of the chasm, rocks crumbling off it. One of the Lizard people behind him gave him a push, and he fell.

The others fell with him, and they plummeted into the creature's mouth. Saliva washed over them, drenching them. Bronwyn gagged. Jayden landed against the side of the monster's throat and tumbled downward. He descended as muscles constricted and relaxed, until they reached a pit at the bottom. Bile sloshed at their feet, drenching them in a substance which smelled like sulfur and worse.

Jayden got to his feet, helping Bronwyn up. Savrin and Menek grumbled nearby. The four of them were together in this creature's belly. It wasn't completely dark, but had a soft glow which pulsed as the pit creature breathed.

"Is everyone okay?" Jayden asked.

"I'm alive," Savrin said.

"This is like the story of Jonah in the whale's belly," Menek said. "We are on our journey, just like he to Nineveh."

'Wasn't he reluctant?" Savrin asked.

Menek shrugged. "Hmm. Perhaps we were reluctant in falling into this creature, much like the prophet, Jonah. And yet God has delivered us." He pointed to a ledge of flesh upon which sat a storage chest. "What's that?"

"We'll see," Jayden said. He trudged through the acidic bile to the chest.

It was old. He was surprised it hadn't been digested over the years, though it was made of a hard, metallic substance, perhaps something the creature couldn't dislodge from its belly.

The chest had a latch, which Jayden struggled to turn, as it had corroded over the years it had been in this creature's stomach. Finally, the latch clicked, and the top popped open.

Inside were several scrolls. Jayden picked up one. It had some strange annotation on it he couldn't read.

Menek peered over his shoulder. "Musical tablature!" he announced.

"Huh?" Jayden asked.

"These are scripts for music," Menek said. "These are scrolls. Ancient ones. You see this circle with a line attached? This is how they showed notes. The placing on the lines signifies the notes. I've seen such markings before. This can't be a coincidence. We're far from where we meant to go. Perhaps the Lord brought us here for a purpose?"

"I'll never get used to this strange prophecy swirling around us. I wish we could sense the right way to go," Savrin.

"How could notes be a key?" Jayden asked, ignoring the talk of prophecy and divine intervention. Whether or not it was the case, they had a task to perform and he would stick to it.

"Your playing has quelled spirits. Music must be the key to defeating the ancient evil."

Jayden nodded. He'd heard words from an acting troupe once, claiming they had knowledge of an ancient playwright, from before the toils of this world, when men walked the stars as gods. *If music be the food of love, then play on*, the words had been. The actor couldn't say where the words had come from, but they certainly held profound meaning.

Menek grabbed as many of the scrolls as he could carry, then handed more to Savrin. Soon enough, they held the entirety of them in their hands. Everyone looked at Jayden expectantly.

Jayden glanced between his friends. "What?"

"A plan," Bronwyn said.

"Why should you think I have a plan? I fell in here as you all did," Jayden said.

"You've gotten us out of pinches before," Savrin said.

Menek shrugged.

Jayden leaned a hand against the wall, forgetting it was the insides of some strange beast—slick with bile and who knew what else from its digestion over years. He jerked his hand back. The walls around them moved, making it difficult to stand. Jayden kept his balance as best he could, gripping onto Bronwyn to help hold her on her feet.

"What was that?" Bronwyn asked.

Jayden snapped his fingers. "A plan."

Savrin chuckled. "I told you."

"We have to make this beast sick," Jayden said.

"Why?" Savrin asked.

"What do men do when they're sick to their stomachs?"

"Vomit." Savrin's eyes went wide. "Oh!"

Jayden nodded. "I think if we kick as these side walls enough, it should irritate the beast."

"Sounds reasonable to me," Menek said, positioning himself by the wall. The others did the same.

"Ready?" Jayden asked, but didn't wait for a reply. "Kick!"

The four of them kicked at the surrounding flesh repeatedly. As they did, the walls rumbled. The beast groaned, the noise echoing all the way down the chamber, the reverberating bass sounds and nearly splitting Jayden's skull. Everything shook. The surface they stood on moved in waves. It became impossible to stand. He fell onto the surface, sticky sludge crawling up his back.

"Keep kicking!" Jayden said.

The four kept slamming their feet against the walls, and soon, more liquid filled the area where they had been standing. Menek and Savrin did their best to hold the scrolls above their heads to keep them from getting drenched.

The bile rose, and with it, the walls constricted, pushing them upward. The great beast made a strange sound, like a *hrrrrk,* and the party shot up through it, rising faster and faster through the beast's throat until they reached its mouth. It had protruded from the pit, facing to the side, opening its giant maw wide to spit them out and onto the ground.

Jayden ducked and rolled as he came to a stop, dirt caking him and sticking because of the liquid substance. He was filthy, but at least he lived. The others rolled to a stop behind him.

It was light out, the scorching sun of the plains beating down on them, drying them quickly. The Lizard people had gone to hide from the hot sun under their rocks.

Savrin was the first to his feet, still holding the scrolls, though the escape had damaged some of them. "We made it, and we have the scrolls. But we should get out of here."

Bronwyn grunted. When she tried to stand, she couldn't put weight on her ankle. She limped until Jayden stood and braced her with his arm. He helped her walk out of the Lizard people's strange settlement and back toward their encampment.

"Do you think our belongings are still where we left them?" Savrin asked.

"I pray so," Menek said.

**7**

Their encampment remained intact despite their capture. Jayden and the others packed as quickly as possible, not wanting to risk the Lizard people finding them again. When they had assembled everything, Jayden helped Bronwyn into the cart. Her ankle still had soreness, and she had trouble walking. Not a good thing to have someone along for an arduous journey with a physical ailment.

Jayden resisted saying *I told you so.*

Menek started the horses going, and they took a hard turn south. His plan had been to evade the Deadlands on their return to Tyril by keeping to the coast, where they could see the water.

"The water's no safer," Savrin said.

"Why not?" Bronwyn asked.

"The Merfolk hunt its shores. They may not take kindly to us traveling along their beaches," Savrin said.

"It beats the plains," Jayden said. "I would prefer encountering Merfolk to another run-in with the Lizard people."

He grabbed his harp from his case and produced it.

"You're going to play here?" Savrin asked.

"I need to practice," Jayden said.

"See if you can decipher the annotation of the ancients," Menek said, whipping the horses into a soft trot.

Jayden leaned his harp against his leg and picked up one of the scrolls. This one had dried, but still had some of the strange monster's bile on it. It unrolled slowly, the pages brittle. The symbols Menek mentioned were there. The monk had told him earlier the notes moved along lines in intervals, explaining what he could about the ancients' writings while they traveled. A line to a space could represent one string movement—and perhaps the different shapes meant time intervals.

Jayden would work with the string movements first, one step at a time, running his finger along the first few symbols. Three up, one down, two more down. His fingers danced along the strings in that order, creating a melodic tone, a hopeful one. As they traveled, he read more of the symbols, playing more of the pattern. After nearly an hour, he'd gotten through the first row on the page, finding himself growing weary from the mental focus.

Taking a deep breath, Jayden played the sequence again. This time, the notes flowed into something beautiful. He had the notes right, but what about the timing? He glanced again. Some symbols had been filled in, others were only an outline. What could it mean? He tried a few variations, but settled on the outlined ones representing double the filled in notes. Once he'd come up with a pattern, Jayden tried again.

"The song sounds wonderful," Bronwyn said.

"The ancients seem to have known their songcraft," Jayden said. "I think I can piece some of these together. Even if we can't use them for anything other than pleasant songs, it will make our tavern playing much better. We can brand ourselves as people who learned music from the ancients. It might carry to nobility in different lands." He still held the dream of being a prominent musician, even if fate diverted him.

"I doubt we'll ever have normal lives again," Savrin said.

Bronwyn frowned, no doubt from the reminder of the life she'd lost as a princess. So much time had passed for her since the Sorcerer

King stole her heritage. She must have no idea where to begin. Jayden wished he had comforting words for her.

The cart slowed. Jayden glanced past Menek to see the reason. In front of them, on the sands, six Merfolk posed erect—blue scales shimmering in the sun, each with a long, thin fin running from the tops of their heads down their backs and disappearing into long tails. Some had spots on their foreheads, others had none, but all had piercing golden eyes.

Menek stopped the cart. "Merfolk. We come in peace. May we help you?"

The Merfolk slithered on their tails to the cart, peering at them in apparent judgment. Bronwyn recoiled, grasping Jayden's arm.

"You trespass on our lands," one of them said.

"We're only trying to get back to our kingdom. The road is too dangerous away from the shore. Please, let us pass," Menek said.

"We have purged this land of humans for generations. Our beaches are pure, except for your presence," the Merman said.

"What would you have us do?" Savrin asked, throwing his hands up in impatience.

"You've already sullied our easternmost beaches. You will be brought before the Mer-King and receive his judgment," the Merman said.

Menek frowned. "There is no way you'll let us leave?"

"No," the Merman said. He jabbed the butt of his spear into the sand as if to emphasize the point.

The others turned to Jayden, putting him in the position to lead once more. How had he become the one to rely upon for decisions? The Merfolk didn't appear overly aggressive, though they dressed as warriors with their spears and breastplates. Still, they had come to talk first and hadn't attacked them on sight like the Lizard men had. This race had some semblance of civilized thought, at least.

Attempting to fight and flee would surely result in injury, if not death, which Jayden didn't want to be responsible for. Moreover, he still held his reluctance to do combat. There had been a lot of violence on this journey so far, but he'd mostly been able to avoid killing his fellow humans.

"We will agree to your demands," Jayden said.

Bronwyn clutched him even more nervously.

"How are we to meet your Mer-King?" Jayden asked.

The Merfolk pointed toward the ocean. Waves beat against the shore.

"Surely, you jest," Savrin said.

"I do not," the lead Merman said.

"We can't breathe underwater," Menek said.

The Merfolk talked amongst each other in their own language. The lead Merman turned back to the party. "We have ways to handle this. Our shaman will take care of you."

"I don't approve of magick," Menek said.

The Merman stared at him flatly.

Jayden pushed himself to his feet and exited the back of the cart. It wouldn't be wise to fight the Merfolk, regardless of their aggression. Other races had their magicks. It was a reality. He assisted Bronwyn out, and Savrin plopped down behind her. The Merfolk surrounded them, bringing Menek in tightly with them, forcing them close together.

The Merman shaman lifted his hands and chanted. The sand moved around them, rushing away from them like ocean waves. Jayden saw soon his feet were no longer on the ground, but he stood on air. The sun reflected light, which shone in his eyes. Jayden turned. A thin and translucent bubble formed around them, disappearing from view unless one tracked it closely. The bubble carried them.

The Merfolk slithered to the water and swam. The shaman lowered his arms, and the bubble moved off of land, skimming over the ocean.

They descended into the depths of the sea.

* * *

THE BUBBLE SHOT undersea with tremendous force. Water rushed all around them, and pockets of smaller bubbles flooded Jayden's field of vision. The number of bubbles grew, until they couldn't see anything at all.

When the bubble stopped moving, fish swam around them, some glowing and producing light of their own. Strange ones lurked the depths with protruding teeth and antennae. They did not look friendly.

A stronger light shone ahead, and the bubble moved toward it, as if attracted by its glimmer. As they came closer, an underwater city became visible, filled with bubbles much like their own, glowing with whatever green substance the Merfolk used.

Their mobile bubble floated toward an area which appeared to have a metallic floor with an oval pad. It merged with the bubble inside the city, and the party fell onto the platform. Jayden landed on his feet, but the others fell. He helped Bronwyn up, and when he turned again, Merman guards surrounded them with spears. The shaman slithered ahead of them.

"To the Mer-King's chambers," the shaman said, leading them along the platform toward a long pathway. All the external bubbles had pathways heading to a center, a structure contained within a bubble itself, where most of the light originated. The structure stood as tall as any castle, with stone and gold intertwined and an aqua-green roofing. To find such under the sea made Jayden's jaw drop with awe.

How many people never ventured this far away from the human kingdoms to even find the Merfolk existed? He'd heard tales of the creatures, but never encountered anyone who'd seen one. It must have been because they kept the shores bordering their underwater city so closely guarded.

Guards opened two large doors which appeared to be made from the shell of a giant mollusk, leading them into a resplendent antechamber adorned with gold, pearls, and gems of the likes Jayden had never seen.

Menek glanced around, seeming to pay particular attention to the city's construction. "Merfolk have gills and lungs, then? Interesting construction, with a full air pocket around this city."

"This city was created by the magicks of the ancients. They called it an underwater observatory," one of the guards said. "We have inhabited it for a long time since and made our own aesthetic changes to make it more suitable."

The party moved inside, making their way through the large room to another where two more guards pounded spears on the ground to announce their presence. The guards opened two golden doors adorned with ornate carvings of merfolk doing battle. Beyond lay a throne room, with a Merman three times the size of the others in both height and girth, with two beautiful Mermaids around him, their breasts bare, save for golden necklaces resting on them. The Mermaids wiggled their tails and laughed while talking with the Mer-King.

Savrin's eyes went wide and his jaw slackened at the sight of the Mermaids.

Jayden nudged him in the side. "Eyes off them."

Menek leaned in. "Anyone who looks at a woman lustfully has already committed adultery in his heart."

"Way to ruin a moment," Savrin said. He shifted his eyes toward the Mer-King.

It would be better. Legend had it, Mermaids could sap a man's soul by luring them in. He didn't know how much stock he put in the tales, but with everything else he had seen as of late, he wouldn't count it out.

"These are the intruders?" The Mer-King said in a booming, deep voice.

The chamber rattled around them.

"Yes, my liege," the shaman said, bowing before the Mer-King.

"Arise."

The shaman raised his head. "They crossed our shores, yet demand safe passage."

"What makes you think you are worthy of setting foot on our sands?" The Mer-King asked.

Menek stepped forward, eyes meeting the Mer-King's in defiance. "We are the sons of God, creator of all things."

The words made the Merfolk in the room flinch. Did the name of God hold so much power with all these creatures? If it could only be so simple with men, it would solve a lot of problems. Jayden would have liked to have crushed the Sorcerer King with mere words, but perhaps because he technically could claim inheritance to the image of God as well…

These thoughts would do him no good. Menek may have made their situation all the more precarious, as the Mer-King's gaze turned into a glare.

"Bold claims, humans. If you are truly sons of the Creator, then you should be put to the test," the Mer-King said.

"We fear no test," Menek said.

"Speak for yourself," Savrin said under his breath.

Jayden agreed with Savrin. Who knew what the Merfolk might torture them with? He didn't relish the thought of drowning in some undersea quest.

The Mer-King examined them in silent deliberation. The Mermaids flipped their tails beside him, trying to woo the attention of the men toward them. Jayden refused to let his eyes drift to them.

"Sons of God should be able to best any of the other beasts of this world in anything, if you truly inherit all he is." The Mer-King clapped his hands together. "I will call my two best warriors, guardians of my throne room, to do combat with two of you. If you survive, you will prove you are who you say you are." He nodded toward the guards. "Take them to a cell until we're ready for them."

JAYDEN WANTED TO AVOID FIGHTING. He had spent the last several years of his life trying to find peace and not engage in the destruction of others. But since Savrin had drafted him and set him on their first foolhardy quest, it seemed violence would not leave him be.

*Lord, what have I done to deserve this fate? Have I not been faithful since my baptism?* Jayden asked in his head.

No one answered.

A Merman guard opened the cell door. "Have you chosen your champions?"

The four companions glanced at each other. They hadn't discussed it since being locked in here. Menek had been deep in prayer, asking God for deliverance. Bronwyn brooded and fretted. Savrin made a few jokes, but they fell flat. Jayden want to talk to anyone.

It had been hours.

But the choice of their champions would be obvious.

Jayden stepped forward. "I will be one champion, and Savrin will be second," he said.

"I didn't volunteer for this," Savrin said.

Jayden shot him a cold look. It silenced the rogue.

"Very well," the Merman said, banging the bottom of his trident on the ground. "You will come with me to be fed, cleansed, and rested before the ceremony."

"Huh, maybe not so bad after all," Savrin said.

Brownyn rushed to Jayden, clutching him by the arm. "Be careful. The Merfolk are strange people, and they are not kind to outsiders."

Jayden met her eyes. She had such deep, shining pupils, and they held genuine care for him. How he wanted to kiss her right here—but it would not be the right time. "I'll do my best," he said.

Brownyn's fingers released him as he joined the Merman.

The guard ushered them down corridors with translucent walls, allowing a view out into the dark seas beyond. Some light trickled from the surface, but strange glowing lanterns created most of it. The lanterns hung along the corridors and lit the inside and the outside. A strange fish with long teeth swam by.

"I'm glad we don't have to go out there," Savrin said.

The Merman turned to look at him curiously. "You will fight in the traditional seabed."

Savrin grumbled.

How would they fight out there? They couldn't breathe water. Jayden hoped all would be revealed in time.

For now, the Merman took them to a dining area, where Mermaids slithered about on their fins along the slick floors, bare-breasted and beautiful. They attended to Jayden and Savrin, bringing them food and wine.

"Would you like assistance in purification? We can rub oils on you." one of them asked.

"Why ye—" Savrin started.

Jayden elbowed him in the side. "No. We will handle ourselves. Please prepare the oils for us and leave us in peace. We are a modest people."

Two Mermaids glanced at each other, eyes large and eyelashes fluttering playfully. They giggled and disappeared from sight.

Jayden finished his food. It had been awhile since he'd had a good meal—beyond their rations or something they found on the side of the road to roast over a fire. The Merfolk had a nice selection of seafood. It left a salty taste in his mouth, quickly quenched by a glass of water.

"I think we can take them," Savrin said with his mouth still full.

"Pardon?" Jayden asked.

"In a fight. These Merfolk are big and strong, but we'll be faster."

Jayden hadn't thought much about the battle strategies. Looking for a way out had occupied his mind. They were too far within the depths, however, to mount an escape. They would need the Merfolk for passage out of here—unless they could find special vehicles to allow them transport to the surface.

Or they could coerce the shaman into making one of those bubbles to bring them up to the open air.

If they tried to capture the shaman, it would lead to a fight against the Merfolk warriors, anyway. They might as well do it in the arena.

He'd hoped for another solution other than combat. His harp had done wonders in helping him to mostly avoid bloodshed on this journey, but it wouldn't solve everything.

Jayden slumped his shoulders, wishing he didn't have to go through with this, but there would be no other way.

"We we should see if there's a way we can analyze our opponents to get an upper hand," Jayden said.

"I doubt we're going to get much information from them. They're giving us a king's treatment. Why don't you enjoy it?" Savrin shrugged.

Jayden sighed. "Just don't do anything foolish."

* * *

THE MERFOLK PURIFICATION chamber comprised a deep half-shell with soft linens and pillows, bigger than any bed Jayden had ever lain in before. Incense made for a pleasant aroma, and it was warm inside. The oils were spread about in smaller shells, left as he'd requested. Outside of the Mer-bubble swam wonders of the deep, some amazing, others frightening. If he never came across the ocean again, it would be too soon. It would have been nice to forget he was there.

The purification ritual relaxed him all the same, the oils and incense the Mermaids left providing a relaxing atmosphere. They'd left him alone in here as he requested. At least they'd respected him that much.

His eyes closed as he let his body relax.

Fingers brushed his shoulders.

Jayden shot upward, eyes opening. The hands pressed on him—soft, small.

"Relax," came a woman's voice. "Don't you want your massage?" Fingers kneaded into his shoulder muscles. It felt good. Too good.

Jayden twisted away from the hands. "No, I do not," he said.

He couldn't help but see the Mermaid in front of him. In many ways, she had the form of Bronwyn, and with bare breasts, much like he'd imagined Bronwyn's would look like, but with a blue skin that blended into the ocean scenery. His breath stilled, and he found it difficult to take his eyes off of her.

The sight aroused him. How could it not? A yearning grew inside of him, a desire to bring her down onto the linens with him. What would it hurt?

She appeared eager, her eyes hungry, her smile bright. Her lips parted ever so slightly, providing an even more sensual appeal to her.

No.

Jayden forced his eyes shut. It would be the only way to avoid her.

"Please leave the room."

"Don't you—"

"Leave me be," he said in a commanding tone.

The woman uttered a soft sigh, and he could hear her slithering out of the room with her tail behind her.

Once the door closed behind her, Jayden opened his eyes again.

Temptations everywhere. This had to be some kind of test. He hoped passing it meant he incurred favor from the Lord. Only time would tell.

* * *

THE CROWD ASSEMBLED in a large bulbous room, with outside water surrounding. Merfolk gathered around the outer bubble surrounding the city, swimming in the waters beyond, peering in at the event.

The shaman uttered something in an ancient language, drawing figure-eights in the air with his hands, which left a strange, luminescent glow in front of their eyes, twinkling until it faded.

The Mer-King slithered forward. "This bubble will collapse soon, and we will enter our hunting grounds to do battle. My shaman has cast a spell which will allow you to breathe in the open waters."

"Wait," Savrin said. "We have to fight in water? You have tails and we do not. It's not fair."

"If you are sons of God, shouldn't your advantage be enough?" The Mer-King asked.

Savrin grumbled. "Stupid Menek."

Jayden said nothing. He stood tall as Merfolk brought them each tridents and shields. He gripped his weapons. They were heavy, but nothing he couldn't manage. Savrin jabbed the open air with his trident.

"This isn't my weapon of choice," Savrin grumbled.

"Stop complaining. They're not going to give us any special treatment," Jayden said.

"You'd be wise to listen to your companion," the Mer-King said to Savrin. "Shaman, let the oceans flow over us."

The shaman uttered another incantation, and the walls of the room shattered like glass, water pouring in around them.

The water moved so quickly, Jayden closed his eyes. It hit him hard, the pressure like bricks until his body acclimated. It went up his nose and into his mouth, giving him the sensation of drowning.

His eyes shot open again. Savrin struggled through the water.

But he didn't drown. Jayden found he could still breathe. Salt water clouded and burned his eyes, but he had to keep them open. Another disadvantage against the Merfolk in this coming battle. The odds would be stacked against them.

The Mer-King and his men swam away. It was impossible to get a sense of true direction this deep in the water. Only the strange, glowing lights the Merfolk held gave him the ability to see. No light descended from above.

Jayden and Savrin swam to follow them, kicking through the water. They slowed the party down, unable to keep up with the Merfolks' tails. The Merfolk waited impatiently, bidding them to move faster.

They descended further into the depths until they reached a soft bed of foamy green algae, where they landed. There were large shells, much like in the purification chambers, but these contained sea creatures, bulbous mussels which opened and closed the shells as they breathed. More creatures, long and slithering and making their own light, swam overhead. Plant life filled the area like a forest, long leaves protruding from the ground and flowing with the current.

Two Merfolk soldiers descended from above, stopping several feet from Jayden and Savrin. They also held tridents and shields. These would be the warriors they faced.

The Mer-King raised his arms over his head. "The champions of the Merfolk shall face the champions of the self-proclaimed Sons of God. Let us begin this momentous occasion. May the victors have a thousand songs of glory sung for them from here until eternity!"

If they won, Jayden would certainly write a song about the occasion, but sizing up the Mermen in front of him, with their muscular chests and arms, he didn't see how he'd stand a chance against them.

Savrin had no levity or jokes, which meant he feared for their lives.

For all the pomp of feeding and purifying them, the Merfolk offered no further ceremony.

The Mermen rushed forward, driving their tridents toward Jayden and Savrin, rippling through the water at tremendous speeds.

The men blocked with their shields. Jayden wouldn't be able to stab with such strength. He retaliated, but he couldn't generate enough force with his trident to make the impact the Merfolk had. Perhaps magicks aided his enemies, which didn't make this a fair fight at all.

The Merfolk circled them, waving their tridents tauntingly. They toyed with him and Savrin, prodding their tridents at them in a teasing fashion several times, and then flipping the weapons over in their hands which cut through the water as if the water had no drag. The two men stood back-to-back, not wanting to leave any opening for the Merfolk to strike. If the Merfolk charged again, Jayden and Savrin would get hit.

"They're faster than us," Savrin said.

"I know."

"They're stronger than us," Savrin said.

"I know."

"You don't have a plan, do you?"

Before Jayden could respond, the Merfolk struck again, forcing Jayden and Savrin to break their defensive posture.

Jayden pulled the Merman facing him away from Savrin. At the very least, he could distract one, keep the odds as even as he could. If either he or Savrin fell, there was no way either of them would survive facing two of the creatures.

A trident met Jayden's shield again. It didn't clang in the water like it would have on the field of battle above. Jayden pushed the shield, using it as a weapon to distract the Merman while he brought his arm around.

This time, Jayden struck the Merman, but with the slow speed of his arm, it created only a small flesh wound in the tail of his attacker.

Judging from the eyes of the Merman, it only made him madder.

The Merman stopped toying with him, rushing him and pummeling him with his full frame. Jayden wrapped his arms around the Merman's torso, carried by the flapping tail which pushed them into the currents. He could hardly see for the speed they moved.

But at least while the enraged Merman pushed forward, he didn't strike with his weapon.

Jayden kept hold of his weapon and dragged the tip of his trident along the Merman's back. Jayden used both of his arms to pull the trident toward him, dropping his shield.

The points dug into the Merman's skin, tearing downward. Blood filled the water. The Merman let out a howl of pain, his arms going slack and dropping his weapons.

The Merman had been too arrogant, and it became his undoing. These Merfolk could be pushed into hasty action—an advantage for him and Savrin.

Away from the light, and with blood filling the water, Jayden could hardly see.

He had to get to Savrin. The rogue could handle himself, but Jayden didn't want to leave anything to chance. He couldn't lose his friend, not now. Savrin set him on this journey for better or worse, and he would see it through.

Jayden grabbed his shield again and swam through the pooled blood, trying to find any visual he could use to get his bearings, hoping he went the right way in the depths.

As he came through to what seemed like clear water again, darkness surrounding everything,he saw soft lights in the distance. They were fuzzy, but enough that he found his bearings.

A giant fish swam in front of him.

The same type with the teeth he saw from the Merfolk's domain, swimming outside. He'd been safe then. Not so much now.

The fish noticed him, flopping its tail to come about toward him.

It opened its jaws.

Jayden ducked aside, barely making it safely away from the creature. It didn't move as fast as the Merfolk, but it still could outpace him in water with its fins.

The fish chomped, wildly veering back and forth. Its face slammed into Jayden's body, pushing him backwards.

On its second bite, Jayden held up his shield, ramming it into the creature's mouth. The motion saved him from becoming easy prey for the creature.

Giant teeth smashed the shield into pieces. It broke in the water, the fish spitting it out like Jayden imagined it would his bones. The thought chilled him.

He didn't have time to think or worry. He had to move out of the way of yet another attack.

This time, Jayden peddled his feet to the side. The fish's large tail crashed into his torso, knocking the wind from him. ·

It was an odd sensation, gasping for air underwater. The Merfolk spell held, but he could feel the water go up his nose,. It took him a moment to recover, at which point he found himself face to face with the large fish again.

As the fish charged, Jayden noted it had to move to the side, swiveling its head toward him. The fish didn't have eyes in front—they were on its sides.

He could use this to his advantage, but how?

The fish came at him for a third time. Jayden pushed up, spreading his legs. When its maw closed this time, his legs straddled its top ridge. Its skin had a slippery texture, and he wouldn't be able to hold on for long. In a desperate move, Jayden brought a fist down on the fish's left eye.

The fish reeled in pain, bucking Jayden from his position. He had to go for the other eye, make it unable to see.

But the fish turned around, redoubling its efforts to attack him. Jayden couldn't escape its teeth this time.

He winced in anticipation of the pain coming soon.

But it didn't come.

Red rose from the fish—blood, much like that of the Merman Jayden had slain. The fish jerked and struggled, more blood seeping from it, and then it went limp, rising in the water.

When it ascended, a pole came into view, followed by a person holding onto it—Savrin.

The rogue pulled his trident out of the fish and swam backward to survey his work. "You're lucky I was here! What a beast!"

Jayden chuckled. "I am, indeed. I thought I was coming to rescue you."

"No need. I dispatched the foul Mer-creature within moments. He was overconfident, rushed me, and I simply held my trident forward and waited for him to plow into it." Savrin shook his head. "You should have seen the faces of the Merfolk. They couldn't believe one of their own had been dispatched so quickly. The only question was what happened to you. Your Mer-soldier go down easy?'

"I wouldn't say that," Jayden said. At one time, he had been a great soldier, but he'd done everything he could to only use violence as a last resort in recent years. He had been forced into such situations far too often, but Savrin often appeared the better fighter because of Jayden's lack of practice. It almost made him long for the days when he trained as a fighting man, but he knew he had another path to go down. His adrenaline wore off, making him somewhat weary. All he wanted was to curl up and sleep.

"Let's get back and tell them to be in awe of the true Sons of God," Savrin said, flexing his bicep.

Jayden rolled his eyes, and they swam back to the fighting grounds.

* * *

THE MERFOLK HAD A BRIEF CEREMONY, wrapping necklaces of seaweed around Jayden and Savrin. It didn't look or feel the most appealing, but Jayden understood it was of importance to these people, so he didn't protest. Menek and Bornwyn were brought out to join them, and it seemed the Merfolk treated them as guests rather than prisoners.

They played songs on strange shell-based instruments in Jayden and Savrin's honor, ones they written for their victory.

While it was enjoyable, Jayden yearned to play music for himself. His harp was back on the surface, and they had to get back. Danger loomed above, he could sense it, and he had to be there to face it.

Still, he enjoyed the festivities as best he could. They ate, enjoyed song and dance, and Savrin drank enough libations for the both of them.

The Mer-King gave profuse apologies, but Jayden told him he needn't. It only seemed to further impress the underwater monarch.

"You are magnanimous, Son of God," the Mer-King said.

"I'm only concerned with moving forward. There is a great evil coming over the lands above, and we are tasked to fight it."

"There have been prophecies of such from the pearl-seers," the Mer-King said.

"Have there?" Jayden asked.

The Mer-King nodded somberly. "We couldn't be sure, but after you dispatched our finest soldiers, I could see they were true. You are chosen."

"I'm just a soldier who understands combat," Jayden said. "And I don't want to see more of it. I want peace in our time."

"Perhaps peace with the overworld is something we can attain," the Mer-King said. He frowned, glancing downward. Then he looked back up at Jayden. "I've resolved to come with you. I'll escort your party against this great evil and lend the strength of the Mer to your side."

Jayden hadn't expected the Mer-King to make such a gesture, nor did he know what to make of it. "I'm honored."

"We will rest here tonight, as you've had a trying time," the Mer-

King said. "I can see you are eager to leave. Then we can be on our way. Everything my kingdom has…" He motioned to several dancing Mermaids, their breasts shaking on their topless forms. "…is yours."

"Thank you," Jayden said, veering his eyes away as soon as they'd fallen upon the Mermaids. He wouldn't succumb to the temptation. "How should we address you? We can't very well keep calling you *king* on the surface."

"I suppose not," the Mer-King said. "Few use my true name, but you may have it. You may call me Floryn."

"A pleasure to meet you," Jayden said, stretching out his hand. He'd been upset by the prospect of being brought down to the underwater Mer-kingdom, but the Lord worked in mysterious ways. This had to be part of the plan. The Mer-King had mentioned a prophecy, much as the monks had before. They had to be related. But what could the divine plan be?

Floryn shook his hand.

Jayden looked upward to the dark waters above.

"Come, let us return to the festivities," Floryn said, patting him on the back.

8

ONCE ON THEIR WAY AGAIN, JAYDEN HAD AMPLE TIME TO WORK ON THE song of the ancients. He rode on the back of the cart through the sands, and with Floryn riding in the cart with them and presenting his seal, the other Merfolk left them alone throughout the entire trip.

Reading the ancient script made Jayden's brain hurt. His eyes glazed over several times during the process, but he had to keep at it and ensure he could play this song. It would be important, he could feel it.

He placed his hands over the harp strings, the frame between his legs. The cart rocked, making it difficult to keep stable. It would have to do.

From the best of his memory of the ancient script, Jayden played.

His fingers danced across the strings, the notes flowing through him, though he played at a tempo much slower than the original piece intended. He could feel it, but he also needed to make sure he played the piece right before bringing it to speed.

The song had a soft escalation, starting in a major key, moving to a minor, the melody rising up the scale. The sound swelled, reminding Jayden of epic ancient battles, the vastness of the world and the stars beyond, and something celestial. The song brought a chill to him, goosebumps raising on his arms as he pressed forward through it.

"This piece is beautiful," Bronwyn said, her eyes sparkling.

"Not compared to you," Jayden said, unable to help himself. It was silly of him to say, but he meant it. He could stare into her eyes forever and never get bored.

She flushed a bright red, bringing even more beauty to her cheeks.

The moment proved too distracting, and Jayden missed the next chord transition in the song. He didn't know it well enough to play through mental lapses.

Jayden sighed, stopping his playing.

"No, don't stop on my account," Bronwyn said.

"Ugh," Savrin said from the other side of the car. "Can you two just get it over with?"

Jayden raised a brow at Savrin. "It?"

"You know… *It.*"

Disgusting. Jayden could hardly believe Savrin would be so crude, though the man had voiced similar with the Mermaids. Fortunately, Savrin didn't seem to have been so foolish to have acted with any of them, despite his bravado.

"We are unmarried," Jayden said firmly.

"Get married then. Menek can perform a ceremony. I'm sick of seeing you two with your glances." Savrin made a ridiculous face with wide eyes and pouty lips. "And your flirting. It's tiresome. And it reminds the rest of us that there are no other women on our journey. A man has needs, you know."

If Bronwyn's cheeks had flushed before, they turned a beaming red now.

"You shouldn't be talking this way in front of a lady," Jayden said.

"Lady. She's one of us. She's been on an adventure this whole time. It's not like there's any secrets in this small wagon. I can smell everything."

"We mostly smell *you*," Floryn chimed in, still looking out into the plains they passed as if they were majestic. From his perspective, the scenery must have been a strange wonder indeed.

"She's still a lady," Jayden said. "And marriage wouldn't make sense now. Not with such darkness. We don't know what the morrow will bring, and I wouldn't want to turn Bronwyn into a widow. It would be selfish of me."

Bronwyn opened her mouth, but closed it again. Her eyes shone at him, as they regularly did.

"It is wise to wait indeed," Menek said. "We need miracles, and abstinence and celibacy will be the best way to incur the Lord's favor."

Jayden nodded, content with his assertion. The monk agreed with him, as he knew the man would. His course would not be his own choosing. Bronwyn offered more than enough temptation. He wanted nothing more than to have her. But the Lord required him to be stalwart.

"There's a castle up ahead," Menek said, changing the subject.

All of them turned to see a dark castle made of stone up on a hill, looking as if it had been abandoned some time ago.

They hadn't made it to the Freelands yet. Jayden couldn't recall the historical peoples who dwelt in this area. From the design of the castle and its state of disrepair, it had been built a long time ago.

"I bet it was a beautiful building, once," Bronwyn said.

"There might be old treasures inside," Savrin said.

Jayden narrowed his eyes at the castle, taking its visage in, focusing on its towers. "I don't think it'd be a good idea to loot this place. Something about it gives me a bad feeling."

"Scared of entering a foreign place on a quest with me?" Savrin asked.

"All of your adventuring hasn't ended well for me so far," Jayden said.

"Chicken."

The conversation died as they came closer to the castle. Jayden got back to his harp playing, working on another rendition of the ancients' song. This time, he played the notes much more smoothly. The music stirred him. This was how they had meant the song to be played. He'd done it right.

The carriage rattled like they were going over a large bump. Jayden struggled to hold onto the harp.

"Watch your driving up there!" Savrin said.

"It's not me. It's the ground!"

Jayden looked up, noticing they'd stopped moving, but cart still shook. The ground moved in waves around them, tall grasses shaking. More, the castle rumbled, its stone unable to take the stresses of the movements.

The towers cracked, large pieces of the castle falling to the ground. A fissure opened along the ground, widening at the castle.

"Methinks this results from your playing," Floryn said.

"How can you tell?" Bronwyn asked, concern on her face.

"My people are more in tune with the world than you humans are. The ground is crying out," Floryn said.

The trembling continued.

It seemed like it would never stop. What had Jayden unearthed? Did the ancients have magicks within their songs which could destroy this world? Would the ground fall apart at the seams and swallow all of them?

Bronwyn gripped the side rails of the cart, her knuckles turning white. Fear filled her eyes.

Jayden wished he could comfort her, but he couldn't say he felt any more secure. Part of him wanted to hop out of the cart, but the ground offered no safety, the way it cracked and opened ahead of them, moving much like the waves of the ocean.

Finally, the shaking stopped.

The party breathed sighs of relief.

Savrin hopped out of the cart.

"Where are you going?" Jayden asked.

Savrin pointed to the castle ahead of them. "Look, it's split in two, opened right up for us. It must be a sign from God. Whatever's inside is ours now!"

"Wait!" Jayden shouted, but Savrin trudged ahead, up the hill along the enormous crack in the earth which led to the split castle.

The building had opened neatly, right down the middle, towers leaning to either side. Some stone crackled and fell from the strain of what they had just endured, but it settled with a little dust rising into the air.

Jayden cursed under his breath and scrambled from the cart.

"I don't think the sign is what he thinks it is," Menek said, joining Jayden.

"No, I don't believe it is, either," Jayden said.

* * *

JAYDEN and the others caught up to Savrin, and then they trudged up the hill together. With all the ground movement, it had left holes and tiny cracks in the ground, as well as raised areas which made it difficult to cross the terrain quickly.

Once atop the hill, they stopped to catch their respective breaths. Jayden surveyed the damage to the castle, which looked extensive. Full stones had been dislodged from their places. Cracks ran down the walls beyond the large gaping one in the middle where the castle had split in two.

The gate fell over from the damage, allowing entry to anyone who dared.

"Looks safe now," Savrin said.

"Famous last words," Jayden said.

"Aw, come on. Don't be such a downer. Things might finally go our way." Savrin pushed forward, stepping over the gate.

"You're forgetting we have an important mission on behalf of the Church Vigilant," Jayden said.

"It'll wait a bit."

Floryn had to move the most carefully, having a long tail to slither on rather than just his feet. Menek stayed with the Mer-King to help brace him over the worst of the bumps. Jayden went ahead with Savrin, Bronwyn joining them.

The girl already had a sword drawn.

"This place looks abandoned," Jayden said.

"I want to be safe," Brownyn said.

He couldn't blame her.

The strange angle of the castle's broken structure cast shadows through the main courtyard. It created an eerie air, further compounded when the wind picked up, gently blowing across the walls, whispering and echoing into the empty place.

The sound reminded Jayden of fighting the banshee on his first outing with Savrin. Another misadventure the rogue had taken him on.

"We should turn back," Jayden said. "This place must have been looted a thousand times over by now. We're not going to find anything of value."

"The shaking might have opened secret passages, or who knows what else?" Savrin said. He explored the courtyard, scanning every nook and cranny to see what he could find.

The man could be so excitable. Jayden understood they had more important matters to attend to. Wasting time here wouldn't be fruitful, even if they didn't encounter any danger.

Jayden also knew the rogue could be downright stubborn. Nothing could make him turn back now.

A strange sound echoed through the courtyard. A rattling of sorts.

The party froze, eyes shifting. Jayden held his breath to listen for the noise.

Given the layout of the courtyard around the inner buildings, it would be possible to trace the source of the noise.

As soon as it had begun, the noise stopped.

Savrin frowned. "Must be some settling from the shaking."

"What if a quake happens again?" Bronwyn asked. "Walls could collapse on us."

"Unlikely," Menek said. "In our records, violent ground shaking rarely hits multiple times. Unless there's a magical source."

The magical element worried Jayden. If some sorcerer had holed up in here alone, he wouldn't be friendly to the party. With all the magick his party had encountered already, he could go the rest of his lifetime and be perfectly content without seeing more.

"Let's just go inside the king's chambers, see what we can find, and we'll come right back out again. Okay?" Savrin glanced at all of them.

Jayden motioned forward. "You lead the way."

They walked down the center pathway, leading to a large door which still hung, even though the structure above it had split apart. Savrin pulled on the handle of the door and tried to open it, but it held shut.

"Shaking must have jammed the door," Savrin said.

"Maybe it's a sign," Jayden said.

"Nothing a little hard work won't cure. And maybe a little leverage." Savrin unsheathed his sword and put it into the door handle. He pushed on it, the hilt just on the corner where it protruded. The door creaked. Savrin grunted with effort, the sound echoing through the courtyard.

The strange rattling sound came again.

The door popped open, Savrin nearly falling over from his effort. His sword dislodged from the door handle, and Savrin dropped it, rather injuring himself grabbing the falling blade.

It clanged on the stone below them.

Darkness lay beyond the door. No torches had lit the hallways of this castle for a long time. Some light trickled through, a thin beam where the castle had split above, guiding their way ahead.

The party tiptoed forward, more cautious than before. The wind eerily whistled through the walls, making Jayden's hair stand on his arms. He kept his hand close to his sheathed sword.

The ground shook again.

Bronwyn braced herself against Jayden, causing him to stumble and push his hand against a wall to hold both of their weights.

Savrin backpedaled, the stone floor in front of him crumbling. The earth seemed to swallow it whole as a large pit opened in front of them, the edge expanding closer and closer to their feet.

Menek and Floryn scurried to either side of the giant hole. The floor fell out from below Menek, but he leaped and grabbed ahold of an old torch-holder on the wall to keep himself from falling.

"Menek!" Savrin shouted.

"I thought you said it was unlikely for another quake to occur?" Floryn asked.

"Only if it's natural," Menek said, struggling to say the words while holding on for his life.

Which meant these quakes had a mystic element to them. Jayden unsheathed his sword, readying himself to fight whatever sorcerer caused this unholy destruction.

None seemed to be in sight, but darkness loomed in the hallway ahead.

The shaking continued, ceiling collapsing in on them. Jayden dodged some of the material falling close to them, bringing Bronwyn with him, tackling her to the floor in the process. He landed atop her, trying not to put his weight on her, but his face came close to hers. Even in the darkness, her eyes shone.

His heart thudded in the brief moment he enjoyed there.

But he couldn't allow himself to fall into such pleasures. Not when they had far too much to do.

Jayden rolled off of her, pushing himself to his feet, keeping his sword blade tucked away from any potential of harming the princess. When he looked up, something rose from beneath the ground.

The rattling sound came along with the ground shaking now.

Beady red eyes glimmered ahead of them, along with a silky snout which glinted in the small ray the sunlight made through the cracks in the ceiling.

The head rose, larger than any man present—including the large Floryn. Its tongue wriggled from its mouth, flapping in front of them. Its neck rose toward the remnants of the ceiling, continuing to undulate upward.

"A giant snake!" Savrin shouted.

Then, the snake struck.

* * *

JAYDEN RUSHED AWAY from the giant snake as it nipped at them, its face crashing into stone, causing the rocks of the castle to rumble like the shaking they'd seen before. Now they knew where it originated—something unnatural indeed.

They hurried out into the courtyard.

"Split up!" Savrin shouted. "It'll confuse the beast."

"Will it?" Floryn asked.

Menek swung from the torch holder, repelling off of the wall and landing safely on his feet beside the Mer-King. "We can pray," Menek said.

Jayden had no idea, but it sounded good. He went left into the courtyard. Savrin went right. Bronwyn stayed with Jayden, while Menek and Floryn followed the rogue.

The snake darted after Jayden.

Its fangs sank into the back of Bronwyn's tunic, tearing into the fabric. She screamed, the sound echoing through the empty courtyard.

Jayden looked back, waving his sword at the creature. It did little other than to make it angrier.

The snake hissed and butted its head against Jayden, causing him to tumble to the ground.

Bronwyn kept running, reaching one of the side doors to the castle tower. Jayden winced from the pain of falling on the rock, but then got back up and followed the princess.

Jayden wished he had his harp on him. Perhaps he could have played a tune to lull the creature to sleep or use it in some other supernatural capacity. The harp had been his saving grace more than once, but it was impractical to try to always lug it with him. It would offer no solution to this crisis.

Something he would have to change—if he survived.

Bronwyn pushed the door open. Jayden rushed in after her. She slammed the door right into the snake's face as it snapped at them again. It hissed angrily, knocking its head against the door repeatedly.The door shook, dust to unsettling around them.

Bronwyn sneezed.

"God bless you," Jayden said.

"Thank you," Bronwyn said. She looked at him with fear in her eyes. "What do we do?"

The door shook again.

"Run up the tower and put some distance between us and that thing," Jayden said.

Bronwyn nodded and hurried up the stairs. Jayden followed, the stairs spiraling around the circular tower, leading them higher and higher. The room trembled even as they moved. A *crack* echoed from below.

"The door won't hold much longer," Jayden said.

Jayden reached the top, with Bronwyn on his heels. From here there was a small opening with a hatch where they could make a stand. A defensible position. The only problem was—they were trapped.

Bronwyn clung to him, her face pressed into his shoulder. "Oh, Jayden."

"I'm sorry, Bronwyn. I should have never let Savrin come into this castle."

"He ran off. You couldn't have helped it," Bronwyn said, clutching him tighter.

Jayden patted her on the back. "I could have been firmer. It doesn't matter now. What's done is done."

The castle tower lurched as the snake crashed through the door. The rattling grew louder as it came up the winding steps, forcing its way through. Its thick hide scraped across the stone.

Jayden pulled back from Bronwyn, grabbing his sword. He would make his stand and would go down fighting. It would be a noble death. The Lord would look kindly on him in the afterlife for his service, wouldn't He?

The snake's thin tongue searched the top of the platform, spit washing the stone floor. Its tip came slithered near Bronwyn's legs.

The woman stomped her foot on the snake's tongue. The creature recoiled, hissing louder than before.

It jammed its head into the aperture below them, squeezing upward, its massive form struggling to push through the spiraled stairs. Jayden jabbed his sword toward the snake's skin. It clanged against its snout, as if the snake's hide were made of metal.

If he couldn't penetrate the snake's skin, what hope would he have? Perhaps he could save Bronwyn yet.

Jayden glanced around the loft, open windows allowing an exit from the tower, but a steep drop to the ground would follow it. He wasn't willing to take the risk by jumping just yet, having already been in the belly of a strange beast and also having lived to survive it.

The snake chomped its jaws, but stayed below rather than pushing forward. It wiggled as best it could, but it didn't come any closer to Jayden and Bronwyn.

Its scales tensed, blood-red eyes narrowing. Try as it might, the snake couldn't move. It had gotten its head stuck between the walls of the opening to the top landing.

The snake couldn't move forward or backward. Slithering up the tower had completely immobilized it.

"Your plan worked!" Bronwyn shouted.

Plan? He'd had no plan of the sort, but the woman looked at him as if he had been responsible for Savring her life. Jayden couldn't find any reason to shatter her heroic illusion of him. He smiled weakly at her. "Yes. But unfortunately, we're trapped here with the snake."

Jayden moved over to a window, glancing outward and down. The drop was at least three stories. They would never make it without some kind of rope. Unfortunately, the landing contained no objects, no chests. All they had was a flat floor meant for a guard to occupy.

He turned back to the snake. The creature looked desperate. It could understand it was trapped.

A sword wouldn't do much. He couldn't pierce its scales. Or could he do something more?

Jayden looked the snake right in its devilish red eyes. Perhaps it had one weakness.

He lifted his sword and struck into its eye.

Blood gushed from the eye, the snake howling in considerable pain. It almost made Jayden feel for the creature, if it hadn't been trying to kill them since they'd arrived here. Its tongue slapped at

Jayden, stinging him. But Jayden could handle a little pain. He drove the sword further into the creature's eye.

The snake thrashed and wailed. Jayden pushed yet harder, trying to drive the point into the creature's brain.

Finally, the snake stopped moving. It went limp, dying in the hallway.

Bronwyn had her face turned away, her skin white as a ghost. "I'm going to be sick."

"Killing gives me no pleasure, either," Jayden said. Even though this creature was an infernal beast, he hated taking its life.

"Hey!" A loud shout came from below.

Jayden again went to the window, looking out upon the castle courtyard. The place had seen such destruction because of this creature, but at least no one had been hurt. At the bottom stood his other three companions—Savrin, Menek, and Floryn.

Savrin waved his hands. "I knew you'd make quick work of the snake. My old unit man comes through again!'

"I was hoping it'd chase after you," Jayden said.

"Well, let's all be glad it didn't. We might have lost Menek if it did."

They all shared a laugh, a pleasant release after the heat of battle they'd just faced.

"The snake's caught in the stairway and there's no way out. Do you think you can pull it free?" Jayden asked.

Floryn inclined his head. "None may match the strength of the Mer-King. We will pry its carcass loose."

The three men below did as Floryn said, though it took more effort than the Mer-King's boasting implied. Jayden and Bronwyn had to push on the giant snake's head from their end to knock it loose.

The men heaved the snake's carcass down the stairs and out of the tower, breathing sighs of relief when they no longer had to shoulder the burden. Now safe, they could take a break before heading back to the cart. Savrin said nothing about uncovering treasure or bringing it back. At least the rogue had *some* sense. This whole diversion into the castle frustrated Jayden, and he didn't want to delve into thoughts about how worthless this escapade had been. It would do no good, and they had to keep moving on.

When they were about the make their way back to their cart, an unnatural darkness overcame the land.

Jayden looked skyward.

Where the sun had been, now a blackness with purple beams pulsing from it hung. The whole land darkened, shadows cast every-where among the hills. Bronwyn gasped at the sight.

"An ill portent," Menek said.

Jayden couldn't disagree. They'd been tarrying too long on their way to the Freelands. Whatever their task, it wouldn't wait for them much longer. Jayden prayed it would be as simple as playing the ancients' song at the proper time, but he had a feeling it would be much more.

"What does it mean?" Savrin said.

"The ancient texts talk about the ground shaking and darkness blotting out the sun when the great demon is free from its binds. He will be loosed upon the world, along with his herald, and only the faithful of the Lord will bring peace."

"Are we supposed to be the faithful?" Savrin asked. "I may have been... less than scrupulous with those mermaids we encountered."

Floryn, the Mer-King scoffed.

"The first step is admitting your sins and repenting of them. Come. Let us waste no more time here. You can confess to me on the way, and I will pray for your absolution," Menek said.

9

After three days' more journey, the party reached the Freelands.

Judging from his last trip to the area, Jayden expected some grand place where men created wonders, but the town they arrived in was in more disarray than the war-torn villages he'd come across during his days as a soldier.

Most of the town was comprised of wooden shacks, poorly constructed and weather-beaten. Dry rot had damaged most of the buildings. Some were in such disrepair that they barely stood erect. A soft wind could blow them over.

The inhabitants of the town didn't look much better—all of them thin and frail. They wore tattered brown robes, and many had scraggly and unkempt hair.

Some did their best to work fields beside the structures, but little grew in the area. Other townsfolk with shaved heads knelt in the middle of the town square, muttering in unison, eyes closed. Prayer.

Upon closer look, the men in the square looked much like the monks Jayden had seen in the Church Vigilant, but worn. Older. Close to death.

The town smelled of death. Or at least animal feces and stale mud. Jayden tried not to breathe through his nose.

His heart wrenched for the Freelands. The port he'd been to on this side of the world hadn't been nearly this bad. What had happened over here? Had they undergone a vicious war, much like the west had endured with the Sorcerer King?

Menek drove the cart into the square where the monks prayed. They remained devoted, not even glancing at the visitors.

"See if someone alongside the road will talk with us," Jayden said.

Menek slowed the horses down, allowing them to pull alongside a man with leathery skin, scraggly hair, and dirt on his face. The man tensed when he saw them stopping.

"Please, if you are a friend of the warlord, only tell the overseers that I am working hard." The man shook as he spoke. "We're far under production, but we've had a famine. Locusts have destroyed many of the crops. We need more time to rebuild."

Jayden hopped out of the cart to greet the man. He kept his sword sheathed, but the man recoiled anyway.

"I won't hurt you," Jayden said. "We don't know of your warlord. We come from the west."

The man turned from the direction they'd come. "Through the Mer-kingdom?"

Floryn slid down the ramp from the back of the cart, revealing his large tail.

The haggard man's eyes went wide. "You come under the protection of the Mer?"

Floryn nodded. "They do."

"I see," the man said, trying to stay cool, but he trembled. "This is ill timing. You should go back from whence you came."

"We have urgent business in the Freelands and we must pass through here. Who is your lord?" Jayden asked.

"You should leave as quickly as possible. Don't ask too many questions. He gets angry when you ask too many questions. The overseers—"

A bugle sounded. Three men on horseback rode to the center of the town square where the monks prayed. They dismounted and walked to the monks.

"The warlord requires your tithe of grain. You've had a full week to comply," the man said.

"That's the overseer," the haggard man whispered to Jayden.

The overseer stood tall, and unlike the others in the town, his belly suggested he'd been well fed. He had a dark beard and shoulder-length hair. One might have mistaken him for a hero if they had been in other conditions.

One monk stood. His legs looked so thin and frail it was hard to believe they could support the rest of his frame. "Please, Overseer," the monk said. "We are praying for the Lord to provide mana from the heavens, as the ground has been unable to provide enough grain since the locusts came."

"I don't care about your superstitions," the overseer said. "The warlord requires results."

The overseer drew a sword.

Jayden reached for his own, but he didn't know the situation well enough to act. In this foreign land, with these strangers around, he could be cut down as quickly as anyone else.

While he hesitated, the overseer struck the monk with his sword. The feeble man collapsed to the ground in front of the others, dead.

The monks wailed, shouting to the Lord for deliverance. The overseer turned away from them, but paused as he spotted Jayden and his party across the way.

Jayden kept his head high as the man came over.

"You're not from here," the overseer said.

"No," Jayden said.

"And you've got strange people with you." The overseer glanced to the Mer-King in particular. "What are you doing in our lands?"

"We are passing through, seeking shelter for the night. I am a musician by trade, and I hoped to get some work at the local inn in exchange for a room or two for my party." Jayden crossed his arms over his chest.

"A musician, you say?" By the way the overseer raised his eyebrow, Jayden could tell the man didn't believe his story.

"I am."

"This town does not have the amenities for the likes of you. The people here are ascetic. Useless, really. They can't even grow their own food properly. They'd rather sit in the square and mutter to their God for deliverance." The overseer huffed. "Their prayers have been in vain so far. Why don't you come play for a better audience, if musicianship truly is your trade?"

"Here will do fine," Jayden said.

The overseer's face went flat. "I do not know if you understand the laws of this land, but when an overseer asks something of you, you would do well to respond positively."

Jayden glanced to the local who he'd been speaking with, and saw the man had slinked away, acting like he didn't know Jayden or his friends. Coward.

No, it wouldn't be charitable to think of a man as a coward. The warlord had subjugated these monks into submission, and the fight had been beaten out of them. ,As Jayden had already witnessed, the overseer met trifles with harsh punishment.

He'd seen this dejection in the Sorcerer King's domain, in the fringe village where his unit used to patrol. The residents there feared the soldiers much as these feared this overseer.

It wasn't cowardice, but a true inability to fight.

"Where would this performance be?" Jayden asked.

"You ask a lot of questions," the overseer said.

"Pardon," Jayden said, uncrossing his arms and raising a hand in peace. "I do not know the customs here as an outsider. We will follow you to where you wish me to perform, and I'm sure it will be enlightening. Yes?"

The overseer grinned. "Much better. Now, come with me."

"I DON'T LIKE this one bit," Savrin said under his breath.

"Nor do I," Jayden said as Menek led their cart up behind the horses of the overseer and his men.

They passed through the raggedy town, onto a poorly kept dirt road, which had grooves from horse's hooves, leaving protruding rocks, making for a bumpy ride.

"Why did you agree to go with them?" Bronwyn said.

"I saw little choice in the matter," Jayden said. "A warlord oversees this area. If we ran, he would have sent men after us. We wouldn't have made it to the next... what do they call countries here in the Freelands?"

"States," Savrin said.

"State, then."

Floryn shook his head. "I will never understand the divisions among you humans. The Merfolk are the Merfolk."

"We're complicated," Savrin said.

"Regardless, we're here. The best we can do is curry enough favor with whoever's in charge here to allow us to move on," Jayden said.

Savrin laughed. "That's ripe. Last time we tried to talk favor, we were forced into deadly combat."

"I apologize for our customs," Floryn said, frowning. "We could not be sure you were who you claimed."

Jayden patted the Mer-King on the shoulder. "It's over now. No hard feelings. I have a feeling this will be different."

Bronwyn stared out of the cart, watching the large castle atop the hill looming before them. "Different. I hope not worse," she said.

* * *

THE CASTLE HAD its servants and decorations like any other, but it felt spartan compared to the domain of the Sorcerer King or that of the Mer-King. No visitors lurked about. Far fewer soldiers stood guard than Jayden would have expected. It wasn't as empty as the vacated castle they'd passed on the way, but it didn't didn't teem with life, either.

Rugs adorned the hallways, preventing echoing footfalls. Light sandstone constructed, this castle and it shone bright under the light of the sun through the windows.

The overseer led them into a chamber with four guards standing at attention, wearing spiked helms and carrying long axes. The few servants occupying the chamber moved swiftly, at least trying to look as if they were busy. None of them made eye contact with Jayden.

The emptiness, combined with their strange mannerisms, created an ominous air to the chamber. Torches flickered on the back wall, casting a shadow upon where two large doors stood shut.

The overseer turned. "You will wait here until we summon you."

Jayden set his harp down, content to not be carrying it, at least for a brief respite. "We'll be here," he said.

The overseer glared at him and turned toward the doors. He disappeared through them soon after.

They waited for a long time. Jayden dared not speak to the others, in case they accidentally committed some social faux pas. How could they know the customs of these people? The overseer had demonstrated an entitled behavior regarding such so far, and he would be quick to violence if someone angered him.

Perhaps the guard wouldn't act in such a manner, but Jayden didn't want to risk it, either.

They remained in silence. A muffled conversation could be heard through the doors. The overseer talked to the warlord beyond—or another of his lackeys. Jayden couldn't be sure of the structure of the leadership here, but he had a feeling there weren't too many layers of bureaucracy, given the small number of servants and guards.

The door opened again with the overseer holding it.

"You may come in," the overseer said.

Jayden now understood their custom of making requests that were truly demands. He motioned his friends forward with his head, picked up his harp, and passed through the doors.

Another chamber lay beyond, with a dais and a throne, where a pot-bellied man with an unkempt beard and oily skin sat. This wasn't what Jayden envisioned at all when he heard *warlord* from the people.

Two guards stood at the back of the room, along with two more on the dais with him. It would be tempting to fight, but Jayden would hear out this warlord first.

The doors closed behind them. The overseer stepped to the dais and took a knee before it. "Majestic One, I present you the foreigners."

"What are your names?" the warlord asked, his voice high pitched.

Jayden introduced his party.

"And you're musicians?" The warlord asked.

"Only I am. The others are from different backgrounds, but we stand together, as there is a great danger over the world which we must overcome."

"Danger, you say?" The warlord frowned. "We've had quite the famine here. It could be a sign of the times. I haven't had my astrologers look into it. Maybe I will." He nodded to a servant in the corner who Jayden hadn't seen before.

The servant wore a robe and disappeared behind the tall throne a moment later. The sound of a closing door echoed through the chamber.

If it was meant to intimidate them, it just made Jayden feel as if this were an odd setup. Did this warlord rule with an iron fist by smoke and mirrors? With ascetic monks, he could have conned them into thinking he was far more powerful than he truly was.

"Yes," Menek said, stepping forward and bending a knee similarly to how the overseer had done. Menek was nothing but proper. "A great evil is awakening. The prophecies foretold it. We must proceed as called by the Lord."

"I am the only lord here," the warlord said. He reached over to the side of his throne, picking up what appeared to be a long stick. Smoke wafted from the end, and he brought the other side to his lips to inhale. Then, he blew out a ring of smoke. "Whatever you think you're doing, you will entertain me now. I demand the musician play."

The others looked at Jayden. These people were awful. Their minor decadence seemed like a plentiful bounty compared to what the monks had in the town below. Couldn't this man see his people were starving? He wouldn't get the crops he wanted if none survived from being malnourished.

But Jayden wouldn't be able to reason with this man. He wouldn't change his attitudes from an interchange of words with a traveling musician.

As the overseer had said, the monks prayed for deliverance. The injustice of it all weight heavily on Jayden. Could he not bring such deliverance here?

Was it his place to interfere?

He didn't know the answer. Slaying these men when they hadn't attacked him seemed wrong to Jayden. He had done everything he could to attain peace in his life. It's why he took up music to begin with. His music might be the answer here. Would it satiate this fat and lazy warlord?

"I'll need a chair," Jayden said.

The warlord flicked his fingers.

A servant appeared again, with a small wooden chair, which the hooded man brought before Jayden.

Jayden sat and situated the harp.

His fingers plucked the strings, playing at first a song from ancient Hyrum, *The Dance of Blades,* a romanticization of early conflicts between Hyrum and the coastal native savages. A great swordsman relied on his faith and felled a thousand—or so the song told. It seemed to Jayden as if the writer had embellished the achievements.

When the song had finished, the warlord kept his eyes fixated on Jayden. He spun his finger around, flicking his wrist. "More."

The word grated on Jayden, but he would continue. Perhaps he could bring peace to these monks below if he gained favor with this man. He played the song of the ancients.

He'd gotten better with the song over the course of the travels, and now could play it flawlessly. The warlord would tell no difference when Jayden made mistakes, but the somber and epic tune carried through the halls. The song stirred Jayden's soul as the calling to play it flowed through him. The harp strings seemed to pluck in time with the rhythm of his heart.

He finished, realizing he had closed his eyes. When he opened them again, he let out a breath. The song of the ancients had been absolutely beautiful. He understood why they saved it for posterity.

The warlord's eyes had wandered toward some fixtures of the room during the song, glazing over. Now they turned back to Jayden. "Your music may be acceptable for an inn, but you do not have the skill to play in the court of the warlord."

Jayden stilled his tongue. He wanted to protest, but angering the man would do no good. Why did this warlord try to goad him?

"Perhaps we should return to the town and find an inn for our companion to play in?" Menek asked.

The monk had a good question, wise and phrased in a way which wouldn't insult the warlord. At least, Jayden hoped.

The warlord grinned. "You have performed work. You may stay here. Overseer!"

The overseer brought his hands together and bowed before the warlord. "At your disposal, Majestic One."

"Ensure these people get rooms. Give them scraps of the bread from our evening meal and water. We will attend to them in the morning," the warlord said.

"Yes, sir." The overseer righted himself, dark eyes meeting Jayden's. "Follow me."

* * *

THE WARLORD GAVE them three rooms. One for Jayden and Savrin, another for Menek and Floryn, and Bronwyn received her own quarters.

Jayden didn't like leaving Bronwyn alone. Given how entitled these men could be, would they desire to take her in an unholy manner?

As much as he feared it, Bronwyn reassured him she would be fine, and noted the warlord hardly looked at her during their time there. It seemed women were of little concern to these men.

Despite her accurate observations, Jayden couldn't help but worry.

He set his harp in the corner of his room, his belt and blade down on an end table beside one of the two small cots.

They were up on the second story. A small window looked out over the castle and the town down the hill. Only a few lights shone in the dark night. The monks of the town conserved their fire—or they had very little means to make any. Either way, this felt wrong compared to his other experience with a vibrant town in the Freelands.

He would hardly call this area free at all.

Savrin drifted off to sleep within moments, a soft snore sounding in rhythm as his breath rose and fell.

The sounds made it harder for Jayden to sleep, who already had too much worry in his head to shut his mind off. They had come here for a purpose, but he believed it would be to find more information on the great evil which would overcome the world.

They'd seen the signs—ghosts, unnatural creatures, men engaged in perpetual war, the blotting out of the sun, the ground shaking and a castle shifting. There could be no mistaking the danger increasing before their senses.

Jayden said a silent prayer for their safety and deliverance—and most importantly, guidance. His party had been meandering lately with little purpose, even if Menek held faith they made their way on the correct path. They'd come to the Deadlands to retrieve the scrolls, but now what were they supposed to do? They needed to avoid the watchful eye of the Sorcerer King, but they couldn't circumvent him forever. There had to be another path.

Once done, he laid himself down on the cot. For a long time, sleep still wouldn't come, as Jayden tossed and turned on the bed, trying to get comfortable. The cot was thin and lumps pressed through the cushion. His back ached no matter how he turned.

Eventually, sleep found him, and he settled into a vivid dream.

*Jayden stood in an underground cave. He had no clothes on, but heat and humidity rose from the ground below. He wished he had some small garment to cover his loins, though no such modesty had been granted him.*

*Granted? By whom?*

*He could hardly remember coming here. This place had a foreign air to it, and it smelled of sulfur. But no others walked the cave.*

*Steam shot upward from a hole in the rock beside him, rattling Jayden to attention. He wished he had a sword, armor...anything.*

*A path cleared in front of him, leading toward a brighter open area. Sharp edges adorned an opening ahead of him, much like teeth or fangs. It made him uncomfortable to pass through it, and when he did, his discomfort grew still.*

*Sweat dripped from his face, but he had to keep going, had to see what would be in store for him on this path.*

*The source of the heat became known as he reached a giant chasm. The place glowed red, and the path ended with a ledge overlooking red hot magma bubbling below, flowing like a river. No wonder it was so hot in here.*

*He'd seen such sights once before—when in the service of the Sorcerer King, Jayden had to traverse a volcano to go to his next battle. His commanders assured him it wouldn't be dangerous unless the volcano erupted, though he couldn't help but want to avoid the sight of liquid hot rock ever again.*

*Now, the substance surrounded him.*

*"There is no way out for you," a gravelly voice whispered within the chasm.*

*No one else stood in the room, yet the voice echoed all around him. Was Jayden hearing things?*

*"I assure you, I am very real."*

*Jayden turned to find the source of the voice, but failed. "What do you want from me?"*

*"To make you an offer."*

*"I only want peace."*

*The voice erupted into laughter. "Peace is not for this world. It never was. The settlers made a grievous error in coming here. They also erred in trying to contain me. No mortal prison can hold a soul, after all. And soon I will divest all of your people of their mortal flesh. Consider it a favor to release you from the struggle of this life."*

*Jayden tensed, realizing who spoke to him. This was the demon the ancients had sought to imprison. The one now being loosed on the world. His memory was fuzzy about how he'd gotten here. Had the demon transported him? Did he fight an infernal being with such power? The Sorcerer King's magicks looked like parlor tricks in comparison.*

*"Give up your search for me. Live the rest of your days in peace. I will allow you to remain until the day comes I must rid this world of the Sons and Daughters of God. I'll even leave the girl with you so you can enjoy her company."*

*Bronwyn. Jayden wanted nothing more than a peaceful life with her. But this demon didn't offer a peaceful life, only a temporary respite. What kind of bargain did he think to make Jayden?*

*"No," Jayden said.*

*"What is it you seek, then? I can make you rich beyond your wildest dreams, give you your own kingdom. Make you the ruler of men under my domain. Would that interest you more?"*

*"I have no wish to rule over others."*

*"I tired of you."*

*The magma below bubbled, a jet of the substance shooting up toward Jayden. He recoiled from its heat, though thankfully the liquid didn't touch or burn him.*

*"I am protected by one greater than you," Jayden said. "In the name of the Lord Jesus Christ, I will vanquish you."*

*The whole cave around him groaned at the words. The voice turned into a loud growl. The magma shot up in a large column, changing course mid-air and flying toward Jayden.*

*Instinctively, he raised an arm to block the hot liquid, even though he knew it would offer him little protection.*

*Just as the magma should have reached him, everything faded.*

Jayden gasped, waking in sweat. What had just occurred?

His eyes shot open, and in good time, as he saw the glint of metal above his head.

An assassin brought down a dagger.

Jayden rolled off the bed as the point of the dagger struck, piercing through the cot's cushion.

Feathers flew into the air when the assassin ripped the dagger out again. It was a man, lithe, dressed in all black and masked, perfectly concealed in the night.

Jayden stood in between the two beds, his belt and blade on the end table on the other side of him, out of reach. He needed to circle the bed to get there. Diving across would leave him too exposed.

Savrin stirred while the assassin followed around the bed to reach Jayden. The rogue didn't make any noise. Smart of him.

When the assassin reached the foot of the bed, he charged Jayden.

Now, Jayden hopped onto his cot and across it, dodging the swings of the man's arm. The point of the dagger tore his nightshirt, but didn't hit any flesh.

Jayden spun, now near to his blade. He reached for it, keeping his eyes on the assassin.

"You cannot win here. If I don't kill you, one of my brothers will," the assassin said.

"We'll see," Jayden said. He pulled his sword from his sheath. Now the fight would be even.

The assassin struck at him.

Jayden parried the dagger with this sword. The assassin could move quicker with his smaller blade. He would have been vulnerable to Jayden's reach, if Jayden had enough space to swing the sword properly. Confined in a corner with furniture around him, all he could do was jab forward.

It made his movements predictable and gave the assassin space to move.

The assassin came in close, grabbing Jayden's sword arm with his free hand. The lithe man had surprising strength, keeping Jayden's sword at bay.

The dagger flashed in the assassin's other hand, pressing toward Jayden, who barely dodged out of the way.

The assassin gasped. He dropped his dagger, loosened his grip on Jayden, and crumpled to the floor.

Another dagger protruded from his back.

Behind him, Savrin stood, rubbing his hands together. "Always getting into trouble, you are," he said.

Jayden shook his head. "*We* are. You're the one who set me on this adventure. But we can't rest yet. He mentioned his 'brothers'. Bronwyn may be in danger."

He took off running for her quarters.

* * *

When Jayden arrived at Bronwyn's room, he found her standing opposite of another assassin as he had feared.

Much like the situation with his own assailant, this man held a dagger and faced Bronwyn with the bed in between them.

Bronwyn gasped with fear. Her expression sent Jayden into a blood rage.

A growl escaped his throat as he charged the assassin. Bronwyn's attacker turned as Jayden swung his sword at him. The attacker knocked the blade from his wrist at the last moment. Jayden wouldn't be deterred, and tackled him onto the bed. The hooded man struck wildly with his dagger, nicking Jayden on the shoulder, but Jayden caught his wrist before he could do further damage.

They struggled for control.

This man had greater strength than the one Jayden had encountered in his own room. It nearly matched his own.

Jayden fell on top of him, but it proved little advantage. Despite how he struggled, he couldn't pry the knife away from the man's hand.

The assassin head butted him.

For a moment, Jayden saw stars. The blow hit him square in the forehead, and the man's skull was as hard as stone. More, the attack caught him off guard. It took every ounce of his strength to maintain his grip on the man's wrist and keep his dagger away.

When he recovered his senses, Jayden struggled with the man. He took an elbow to the ribs, but pressed his knee into the man's groin. Sweat dripped down his face.

Savrin should have been behind him. Where had the rogue gone when he needed help?

The two of them could overpower this assassin easily, but Jayden fought alone—or so he'd thought. Both men had ignored Bronwyn.

She found a large tome, brought it up over her head and slammed it down into the assassin's head. The act seemed not to faze him, but Bronwyn struck again—and then a third time.

Jayden glimpsed the tome, which had metal trim around it. Even from a woman's meager arms, the blows must have done some damage, for the man's eyes had gone glassy.

Bronwyn brought down the book a fourth time.

The assassin lost his grip on the knife. It fell to the bed. Jayden reached out and grabbed it, quickly bringing the dagger to the man's throat.

"Surrender," Jayden said.

The man's lips tightened, but he saw he was beat. "You'll let me go?"

Jayden didn't want to promise the man's freedom after he'd tried to harm Bronwyn, but for the sake of negotiation, it would be the wiser course. "I will if you tell me who sent you."

"The overseer," the man said. "He said you were troublemaking foreigners here to overthrow the kingdom."

Jayden let out a sigh. It sounded like something the overseer would say. The man hardly had a cause to lie. It meant their mere act of being within the castle here was a greater danger than they had assumed.

He let the assassin up.

The assassin stood, making space between him and Jayden.

"If you sound the alarm, I'll kill you," Jayden said.

"We should bind him," Bronwyn said.

"It'll be better for you anyway," Jayden said. "The overseer wouldn't be pleased to see you failed and cowering. If you were overpowered and bound perhaps he will spare you."

The assassin frowned. "I hadn't thought of that."

"Let the woman tie you in sheets," Jayden said, motioning to Bronwyn.

She took the bed sheets, twisting them into a rope, and then bound the assassin with his hands behind his back. She did the same to his feet with the next layer of blankets. He was secure, and they laid him in the corner of the room.

A figure appeared in the doorway.

Jayden turned, ready for battle.

Savrin held his hands up. "Don't attack me, old friend!"

"Where have you been?" Jayden asked.

"You went for this room, so I went to assist Menek and Floryn. Their assassin hadn't entered the room yet. I took him by surprise and made quick work of him. But I woke them so they would be alert."

The monk and the Mer-King appeared behind Savrin.

"Everyone's here," Jayden said. And without a good night's sleep, like he had hoped. But they couldn't go back to bed now. The overseer —or his boss, the warlord—would surely hear of the troubles here and send someone else to kill them.

"We have to get out of here," Jayden said.

"And then what? We'll be in these lands with overseers hunting us down," Savrin said.

"Do you have a better plan?" Jayden asked.

Savrin grinned. "We can be this realm's deliverance—agents of the Lord!"

"Surely, you jest," Jayden said.

"Why not? We'll have better chances taking out this lout of a warlord, and spurring the folk into uprising, than we will if we're on the run. Besides, we've handled worse."

As much as Jayden wanted to argue, he saw merit to the rogue's words. But he also didn't want to risk his people—especially Bronwyn. Had the rogue grown soft over this trip? It was something he'd have to ask Savrin later.

"I agree," Jayden said. "Perhaps our friend here can tell us where the warlord sleeps." He motioned to the bound assassin in the corner.

* * *

THE MORE HE thought about the plan, the more he wished he'd rejected it.

It would have been easier to run from these tyrants—especially in the middle of the night.

The party had horses and a cart. They might have gone unnoticed until morning, at which point they would have such a head start over the warlord's forces.

But, Jayden recalled the downcast faces of the townsfolk, the poor monks who—even though they renounced material possessions—still appeared a meal or two away from starvation.

The warlord had treated them inhumanely. Perhaps God had a plan for them to come this route and take care of business.

A little over a month ago, he would have laughed at anyone who told him he would be an instrument of the Lord. Now, he couldn't find coincidences in any new task life brought him. Everything had a purpose.

His party tip-toed down the corridors of the castle, making their way to where the assassin had told them to go. He had to trust the man told the truth. If he hadn't, they could be trapping themselves.

There was no other option if they wanted to remove this tyrannical leader. Now would give them the best chance to push through the light guard.

The castle looked as dead as a tomb. No moon shone outside, leaving them in complete darkness as they passed windows. Eventually they came to a grand set of ornately carved double doors. This room stood out as more compared to all of the others. This must have been where the king kept his quarters, back when this land had a king.

Jayden motioned Savrin forward. The rogue turned the knob, and the door opened, though with a small creak.

"Who goes there?" asked a guard from the other side of the door.

When the guard entered the hallway, Savrin garroted him with the dagger he'd taken from the assassin.

The guard fell, choking on his blood before he *thudded* onto the floor. Another guard arrived at the door quickly, the bottleneck of the corridor giving an advantage to Savrin, who made quick work of the second just as he had the first.

He waited, but no others came.

Once sure no more soldiers were sneaking up on them, Savrin burst through the door. He checked each side of the door for hidden assassins, and once clear, he beckoned Jayden forward.

The warlord's chamber was dark, with an enormous bed and multiple posts. The portly warlord lay fast asleep on his bed, breath rising and falling with a soft snore. Even the commotion of the guards hadn't stirred him.

No further guards appeared before them.

Savrin moved forward, steel in hand, though only appearing as a shadow with the lack of moonlight.

Jayden took him by the arm. "Wait," he whispered.

"Why?" Savrin asked in a low tone.

"We shouldn't murder a man in his sleep."

"He wouldn't hesitate to do the same to us. His overseer already tried to do the same to us."

"But we have to be better."

"He's a tyrant. We can't just leave him like this. Or wake him up and kill him. What would it matter?"

Jayden didn't know. He didn't feel right about cold-blooded murder, even of an evil man like this.

"Wake him, bind him, gag him, and take him hostage. We can bring him before the monks in the square and let them enact justice," Jayden said.

"They'll cower in fear. We'll draw more of the overseers to them," Savrin said.

"Please."

Savrin shook his head. He moved to the warlord, looking as if he were going to comply with Jayden's orders, but then, at the last moment, he lifted his dagger and ran it across the warlord's neck.

The warlord jerked awake, choking in his final moments before he died on the bed.

Jayden grabbed the rogue by the arm, no longer whispering. "What do you think you're doing?"

Savrin turned, sheathing his blade. "Sometimes war demands ugly acts. If we had left him, we would have done no good here. Now we can show the monks they are truly free and send a warning to the overseers they should get out of this region." He motioned to the others. "Wrap the body and bring it."

Jayden wanted to punch the rogue. He hated Savrin's glib casualness about killing. True, they'd been in war together. He'd seen all kinds of horrors, and always tried to get Jayden to be a leader. Though Jayden had protested, his friend rebelled now that he'd finally accepted his fate?

As they departed the chambers, Jayden's heart sank. How could they save the world if they couldn't keep simple values such as not killing a defenseless man?

He kept his mouth shut, not wanting to lash out and cause further dissension while in a foreign castle. But he would have words with Savrin later.

* * *

SAVRIN PULLED the blanket away to reveal the warlord's body, letting it fall to the dirt in the town square.

The monks stepped back, eyes wide from the brutality of what they saw.

"This is the warlord who gave you trouble. He is no more. The castle is free of many of his guards. The others would do well to flee—same goes for his overseers!" Savrin said.

Jayden hadn't seen the rogue so animated and serious before. Usually, everything came with a quip from him. The monks' plight must have really stirred him.

One monk came forward. "Who will rule our land? Will it be you, Warlord Slayer?"

Savrin chuckled. "I probably should take you up on the offer, but I have other things to do. We're on a mission, one the whole world depends upon us to complete."

The monk opened his mouth to speak further, but his eyes rolled back and he convulsed. Other monks grabbed him by the arms to hold him up. The man thrashed and made strange noises.

Jayden stepped back, not wanting to get caught in the man's flailing. Was a demon possessing him? He'd never seen anything like this.

The seizure passed, leaving the monk limp in his people's arms. They dragged him under an overhang to get him out of the sun. Others brought him a small leather skin of water, dribbling it on his lips. The monk had turned ghost white and could hardly move a muscle.

Bronwyn stepped toward the townsfolk. "Is he all right? Can we do anything to help? Menek has healed ailments in the past."

One man holding the monk upright shook his head. "No. The seizures are a divine gift from the Lord. It means our brother had a vision. We will wait for him to recover to hear what he says."

Minutes passed while the monk regained his composure, drank more water, and returned to breathing normally. His face resumed its natural leathery coloration, and he sighed in relief. "The episodes are getting worse. It is a difficult path to be chosen by the Lord." The monk met Jayden's eyes. "As I'm sure you know."

Jayden lifted his head in acknowledgement.

"My vision pertains to you and your friends. The time draws near. The ancient evil sheds its bonds, and you must be at the appointed place." The monk closed his eyes. "I saw the pits of hell, lakes of fire, unbearable heat."

"I've seen it too," Jayden said.

The monk nodded. "The place... The Demon's Eye. You must head to the shores of the great lake at the center of the world. That is where your destiny awaits."

"What are we supposed to do there?" Savrin asked.

The monk's eyes fluttered open. "The Lord did not grant me such wisdom, only a vision of where you will be. It is all I know." He smiled weakly. "Trust him. He will provide."

Savrin huffed. "Easier said than done."

"But it is the correct path," Menek said. "We've seen enough signs and wonders. The time grows near. We should depart immediately."

Jayden frowned. "Are you sure you'll be okay here? We haven't dealt with the overseers, just their leader."

"When word spreads of your deeds, they will flee. The overseers are cowards, relying on the warlord's word. Without it, they will scatter."

"If you say so," Jayden said. He didn't feel right about leaving them, but supposed he had little choice.

As they settled into their cart to shift their course and make their way toward The Demon's Eye, a shadow crossed overhead. This wasn't like the covering of the sun before—the shadow had wings. When Jayden looked up to see what could have caused such a shadow, he couldn't see anything amongst the clouds. It may have been his imagination, but he couldn't help but fear there was something following them, far worse than anything they'd encountered so far.

# INTERLUDE

Interlude Two

Jayden traveled in silence, watching the road. Hills surrounded them, beautiful greenery everywhere. A peaceful sight, but it didn't soothe him.

This whole trip may have well been a fool's errand. Doubt filled him. How could they be sure this was the correct path? Everything had been happening so fast, they'd taken very little time to stop and reflect and be sure they had the correct course.

If some ancient demon awakened, shouldn't they be forming an army? A small party could hardly be a match for such a creature. They should have done more, instead of wandering across the world.

Then, there was Savrin. The rogue passed the time by sharpening his daggers in the cart. He still had such a propensity for violence, one which made Jayden uncomfortable the more they traveled. They had to address what had occurred in the last town.

"Savrin," Jayden said.

The rogue lifted his head. "Hmm?"

"We need to talk."

The others glanced out the sides of the cart, politely ignoring them.

"Say your piece." He went back to sharpening his blades.

"You killed a man in cold blood."

"Ah, this again," Savrin said.

"Don't be flippant with me," Jayden said.

"We had to end the situation. You saw the results. The monks looked overjoyed. They'll finally be able to take control of their own destinies. We did the right thing."

"It was the wrong way," Jayden said.

Savrin shrugged. "What matters is the result."

Jayden reached and grabbed the rogue by the wrist, stopping his sharpening. "No, what matters is maintaining our souls and our righteousness. I warned you of this before, when we met with the Mermaids. You remember their allure. You succumbed to sin. And you did it again here. We cannot afford to darken our souls for this coming battle. There is too much at stake. You're the one who converted me, Savrin, to get me to believe in these prophecies and the scriptures. Please, as a brother, understand."

Savrin looked like he wanted to punch Jayden for grabbing his arm, but he didn't move. His lips tightened. Would he fight Jayden or would he finally listen to him?

The rogue relaxed and sighed.

"If it means this much to you, I will follow your commands from here forward."

It was all Jayden could ask. He nodded. "Thank you, Savrin. I appreciate your companionship. We'll need to work as a unit more than ever if we're going to survive the coming storm."

Menek looked back from his forward seat. "I will be praying for us without ceasing."

10

They traveled even as the sun set.

Tall grasses lined the path, creating a roadway out of what would have been dirt otherwise. Hoof marks and tracks from other carts lined their path of travel.

Menek broke Jayden's daydreaming. "There are torches up ahead," he said.

"Are we coming to a town?" Jayden asked.

"I don't know this area," Menek said.

None of them did. The Freelands were the opposite side of the world for all of them save Floryn, who had little experience in surface travel.

If they neared a town, it would be good to stop for the night. Jayden hoped he could convince a local innkeeper to allow him to play his harp for a room. It had been a long while since they'd had simple accommodations. Everywhere they went seemed to have greater strife than the last.

This demon's influence already manipulated the world.

When they approached the torches, no town appeared, but a band of soldiers and horses. Jayden moved to the front of the cart to get a better look at this encampment upon the road. In the soft light of dusk, he could see the glint of their armor, but little more.

Once they were close enough to see, it was too late. The soldiers would spot them.

Worse, Jayden noticed the flag hovering over their camp—Hyrum. His old country. What business did they have out this far east?

"We have to turn around," Jayden said.

"I don't have a way to do so without great effort," Menek said.

"Try anyway," Jayden said.

The soldiers came forward while Menek nudged his horses to the side. They didn't want to enter the tall grasses with strange hissing bugs, but they had no choice with Menek's tug of the reins.

The horses protested by bucking their heads and huffing through their nostrils while trying to turn. The cart lurched, not meant to go off the path, and not handling the tight turn well.

They couldn't turn all the way around before the first group of soldiers arrived.

"Get your blades," Jayden said to Savrin.

The rogue already had daggers in hand, ready, as he'd seen the danger from the tabards of these soldiers as well as Jayden had. A unit of Hyrum soldiers approached them. But what could they be doing all the way out here?

"Halt!" one of the Hyrum soldiers shouted.

Floryn already had drawn his trident, ready for battle. "No one orders the Mer-King and the Sons of God! Prepare to be struck down!" Floryn shouted.

Jayden counted how many soldiers they faced. At least five approached them, with more holding the line with tents and horses behind them. He wished Floryn hadn't spouted such words at them.

But wishes did little in the course of the battle. Jayden evened the odds by grabbing his harp. He had lured the Hyrum soldiers to sleep with his playing before. He would try the same song now.

The other soldiers rushed forward with their swords drawn. Arrows wouldn't do much in close range. They attempted to seize control of the cart, two of the soldiers grabbing the reins to the horses and the other two positioning themselves to cut off any potential escape.

Menek hit one of the soldiers with his staff. Bronwyn had a dagger but took a defensive position by Jayden and his harp. Savrin hopped out of the cart, surprising one of the soldiers with his speed, slicing the soldier with a couple of quick moves with his dagger.

Three remained, and then a whole army behind them.

Floryn threw his trident like a javelin, but it was hit by some kind of energy from beyond. The energy trickled outward in a pink pattern of hexagons, surrounding the rear soldiers. The trident fell to the ground.

"The Sorcerer King is there!" Jayden shouted.

"How do you know?" Savrin asked.

"I can see his magicks."

It made his playing all the more important. They had to strike quickly.

A bolt of lightning shot down from the sky, narrowly missing their cart.

Savrin felled another attacker, and Menek made quick work of yet another. The last of the advance party realized his companions were lost and retreated toward a group of reinforcements who lingered a ways behind the cart.

Jayden kept his harp ready, scanning around him to make sure there wasn't a bowman getting ready to lob an arrow into his skull. He took a deep breath as he wanted to be sure he could play his lulling song without interruption.

He peered over the cart to get a better view of their situation. There were at least ten more soldiers, and now a robed man came from the tents. The soldiers made way for him as he moved ahead of them without fear. The Sorcerer King. With his magick shield, he couldn't be attacked.

The Sorcerer King stood in his long robes, his dark eyes glaring at Jayden, face lit by more magic energy. He looked as if the demon they chased had possessed him.

"My quarrel is not with all of you," the Sorcerer King said. "Give me the girl and Jayden the traitor and you can be on your way."

"Fat chance," Savrin said.

Ordinarily, Jayden would wish Savrin to not provoke their enemy into rage, but with the Sorcerer King, they wouldn't be able to convince him much through parley, anyway.

"There are greater evils in the world growing," Jayden said. "Surely with your magicks you can feel it. You're far from your domain. You should be protecting your people."

"A traitor shouldn't tell a king how to lead."

Silence fell, wind blowing through the tall grasses. It wouldn't matter what he said to the Sorcerer King. The results would be the same.

"Don't be a fool. This force I go to face will make your magicks seem like child's play. You have Hyrum. You don't need Bronwyn or me," Jayden said.

The Sorcerer King raised his hands in reply, shooting lightning from his fingertips at their cart.

The horses spooked, taking off running at the thunderous boom accompanying the bolts. The magic energy shattered the back of the cart, one wheel coming off and dragging. Floryn fell from the cart, tumbling into the grasses. Savrin lunged after the Mer-King.

and In their terror, the horses became a liability with their dragging the cart, pulling them too hard across rocky ground, causing everything inside to bounce. Jayden couldn't keep his harp upright. It fell, clanging against the cart, and slid out to the dirt beyond.

"Secure the harp," Jayden told Floryn, rushing across the boulders to try to calm the horses and get them to stop. He managed to snag one of the reins, pulling hard to stop the horse nad keep it from darting away from them.

The Mer-King picked himself off the ground and slithered toward the instrument, but when he came close, the harp levitated into the air. It floated as if it weighed nothing, passing overhead Jayden and the others, and landing at the Sorcerer King's side.

"There will be no distractions this time. No tricks from your ancients' magicks," the Sorcerer King said. "I care not about any divine mission you have deluded yourselves into believing. What I want is the girl and retribution for the embarrassment you gave me and my army. If you come and bring her, Jayden, I will allow the others to leave."

Jayden scanned his friends, considering. He would give anything to protect Savrin, Menek, and Floryn. They'd faithfully fought by his side, even if they'd had some disagreements.

If the Sorcerer King had said Bronwyn could leave with them, he might have accepted the plea, but he couldn't forsake her. What did the Sorcerer King need with her, anyway? He already had control of Hyrum.

"Allow Bronwyn to go with them and I will come peacefully," Jayden said.

The Sorcerer King laughed. "I cannot agree. You do not know her true value, do you?"

Jayden looked at Bronwyn. Her face had an expression of confusion upon it.

"You already have Hyrum. She doesn't give you legitimacy," Jayden said.

"I don't need legitimacy. I am the legitimate monarch of all," the Sorcerer King said. "What I need is her power."

Bronwyn shook her head. "I have no power. You're mistaken."

"Just because you do not know something, doesn't mean it doesn't exist," the Sorcerer King said.

Jayden thought back to the moment they met, when he'd felt compelled to kiss her—the act awakening her from her long slumber and the Sorcerer King's spell. What if the compelling was more than natural? Had it come from her? He'd seen little sign of such from her before, but with all the wonders the party had seen thus far, it didn't surprise Jayden to see another of them developing a connection to the divine. It seemed like she had some kind of an innate power of protection, perhaps some magicks within her.

He moved closer to her, and then spoke under his breath, "Will the soldiers to flee."

"What?"

"Try it."

Bronwyn bit her bottom lip. Jayden couldn't help her further, as he had no idea how to work magicks any better than she did. But if she had power in her, something she could have from her lineage of kings, perhaps it was innate.

Her eyes fluttered closed, and she focused. Her face tightened.

The air grew still all around them, and then pushed out in a circle with her at the epicenter. The wind blew Jayden's hair, causing some to fly in his face. It stirred up dust on the road.

Bronwyn glowed with bright light. An angel. The only thing missing were wings and a halo.

Meaning to or not, the Sorcerer King had tapped into some genuine power in her. Now they would use it against him.

Her energy rippled outward, and as it did, it became stronger. The grasses flattened around the cart, bushes uprooted.

The Sorcerer King's horses reared, whinnying with fear. The soldiers who rode them fell off, surprised by their horses' sudden panic.

"It's working," Jayden said. "Advance!" He called to his companions as if they were a part of his old military unit, though only Savrin understood the brotherhood they'd once shared. Still, these friends had become his new unit, his new family. He found with them he no longer yearned for the days when he fought for an unrighteous cause —now he had a noble one.

God would not let them fail here.

He stayed with Bronwyn as she walked forward, her energy flowing through her.

Spears flew at them, but bounced off an invisible shield surrounding them. With Bronwyn's, they now had a power to rival the Sorcerer King.

No wonder the evil man had chased them so far away from his domain. Bronwyn could lay true claim to the kingdom he'd usurped, and she had the means to take it, where others would fail.

What the Sorcerer King failed to understand was that Bronwyn and Jayden had no desire for earthly kingdoms. A heavenly one awaited them regardless of whether their flesh survived. Regardless, they still had the duty to remove the evil infecting this world.

The Sorcerer King's magicks paled compared to the wonders they'd seen. The wonders they had worked through His power. God protected them through incredible trials. Their faith would prevail here.

Their whole party consolidated around Bronwyn, surrounding the woman who, for all intents and purposes, was their rightful queen. Jayden stood proudly at her side as she advanced one step at a time toward the Sorcerer King.

His army had fallen to her initial blast of power. He'd asked her to make them flee, but she had greater capabilities than the Sorcerer King had imagined. Only the Sorcerer King with his personal energy shield still stood.

Jayden's enemy conjured more power, a well of red light coming from the earth. He drew upon the elements, the rocks and lava, the air and water. His magick wasn't based on a supernatural faith, but a command of the elements here—an attempt to *be* God rather than serve him. This was where he would fail.

A blood rage appeared within Sorcerer King's eyes, glowing with all the power flowing through him. He breathed heavily, sweat dripping down his face as everything he conjured drew heat as well as power.

He pushed his hands forward, sending every bit of energy he conjured toward Bronwyn. A flow of deep, glowing red shot toward them, what appeared to be a mix of his blood and the lava from the earth. Scrapes and cuts could opened all along the Sorcerer King's arms, scars from using the same spell in the past.

The red crashed into Bronwyn's light like a monsoon hitting the shore. Savrin flinched—with so much energy coming toward them, it was difficult not to recoil, but Jayden wanted to demonstrate his faith.

As much as the Sorcerer King pushed, as much as he summoned more and more energy from the ground below and from his own body, he couldn't penetrate Bronwyn's shield.

Bronwyn kept advancing, slow step after slow step. She looked more regal in this moment than ever, her beauty transcending her mere earthly shell.

They hadn't talked faith much before, though Bronwyn had been around the same influences he had. If she didn't believe as they did, she would have surely left them. For anyone without faith, they would have seemed a crazy lot.

Over the course of their adventure, Jayden had grown fond of her reserved nature. Though initially it had been awkward between them, he now found her mannerisms comforting and attractive. He glanced at her out the corner of his eye.

Bronwyn edged closer to the Sorcerer King. As they did, the tyrant trembled. He couldn't maintain the flow of power he'd been directing at them.

His body shook, his arms wavered, until finally Jayden and his companions came with a few steps of him. There, Bronwyn stopped.

The stillness of the Lord filled everything around them.

The Sorcerer King's earthly power meant nothing here. It was empty, small compared to the power of eternity, the power of omnipotence.

The energy the Sorcerer King had been summoning dissipated. Spent, the wizard collapsed to his knees. Tears streaked down his cheeks. He cried like a small child, whimpering.

If someone had told Jayden this would of the end of the brutal monarch, he would have laughed at the messenger.

But here, he bore witness to the complete brokenness of the evil tyrant before him. Without his armies, without his magicks, he became a frail man. A speck in the eye of the infinite, just another of God's creations, flawed and corrupted by the true devil.

Menek prayed, rocking on his feet as if in a trance.

Bronwyn continued forward. She crouched before the Sorcerer King, once the strongest, most powerful man in this world, now a withered shell. He'd pulled too much power from the earth and run it through his body. Men were not meant to wield such magicks, a challenge to the divinity of the true God. The total hubris of enacting one's own will on the world.

The Sorcerer King paid the price.

His face had age lines on it, cheeks drooping. Where his powers had kept him young, the lack now revealed an old man.

Jayden frowned, pitying the tyrant despite his burning hatred for the Socerer King.

Bronwyn placed a hand on his shoulder. She looked him directly in the eye.

The Sorcerer King opened his mouth as if to speak, but he choked on his words.

"Worry not," Bronwyn said. "I forgive you."

The pure white energy burst all around her, blinding everything in sight. Jayden recoiled, trying to maintain his footing as the ground trembled beneath him. The sudden shake brought him to his knees.

He shouted, but couldn't hear anything. The energy pushed all sound aside. His ears rang, and he winced from the blinding light.

Jayden brought a hand forward in faith—with his eyes and ears not working, he hoped he could use touch to get his bearings. Warmth surrounded his hand and arm and then enveloped his entire body.

Reality blinked.

His eyes remained closed, but the surrounding light disappeared, as did the warmth. Everything cooled. Jayden opened his eyes.

He'd returned to the path on the road to The Demon's Eye. The sun rose in the distance, soft red light on the horizon.

They'd lost the entire night to whatever had just occurred. He could no more explain what had happened than ascertain its meaning. Perhaps Menek would know.

Jayden pushed himself to his feet, trying to find the others.

He first saw Bronwyn. She lay beside him, asleep, her lungs rising and falling with each breath. She looked so peaceful there.

The Sorcerer King had disappeared. In his place stood a mound of ashes. Whatever had occurred sapped the humanity from him.

Or had it? Bronwyn mentioned forgiveness. Perhaps he repented with all he did and shed his earthly body.

Jayden hoped the tyrant found redemption. It would not be for him to judge but he would find out in the world to come.

He leaned over to gently touch Bronwyn's shoulder.

She stirred.

Her movements came gracefully, beautiful as everything else was about her. She stretched her back and her eyes fluttered open to see Jayden.

"We're alive," she said.

"Yes." Jayden offered his hand.

She took it, and he assisted her to her feet. When she rose, she came close to him, her body against his, her breasts pressing against his chest.

Jayden's heart pounded.

"It's a miracle," Bronwyn whispered.

"Yes," Jayden said.

"What the devil just happened?" Savrin asked from the tall grasses. He poked his head up. "Aw, not again. You two *really* need to get your own room."

Jayden chuckled. "I'm glad to see you, as well, old friend."

Menek popped his head up from the grass, as did Floryn. Everyone was accounted for. There were no sign of the Sorcerer King's soldiers.

"What just happened?" Savrin asked.

"The Lord provided for us. A sign we are on the correct path," Menek said.

"Did you not see the hand guiding our enemy?" Floryn asked.

The entire party looked to the Mer-King.

"I can't say I did," Jayden said.

Floryn frowned. "Perhaps we Merfolk see on spectrums you cannot. Our enemy did not act alone. He was being controlled—until lady Bronwyn broke the hold over him."

"Like a puppet, and she cut his strings," Menek said.

"Makes sense," Savrin said. He kicked at the pile of ash where the Sorcerer King had been. "No human could have been so vile and thirsty for war."

"It's over now," Jayden said. The past would no longer haunt them.

They were truly free of the tyranny. The greatest weight of Jayden's life had been lifted from his shoulders. "I think I know what was controlling him, though. And if this demon can take control of men, we need to be vigilant."

"And we will," Bronwyn said.

Jayden took her hand and squeezed it. He worried about the next fight, but Bronwyn reminded him to relish in the victories. Being here together was a miracle. They should enjoy it while they could. But they had to keep going.

"Let's find an inn and rest awhile," Jayden said.

"Finally, you speak sense. I could use for a pint of beer. Or five," Savrin said.

"Me as well," Menek said.

Jayden turned back to the cart, surveying the damage from the battle. It looked like they would have to take a long walk to the next village and find shelter there.

11

JAYDEN STEPPED OUTSIDE THE FISH HOOK INN, A QUAINT PLACE IN THE shape of a fishing hook, or so Jayden was told, as the innkeeper had escorted the party to their rooms.

Now outside, he caught a different view of the lakeside town. The area looked like it'd been hit a severe storm. Puddles littered the streets, windows were boarded over them, and roofs had caved in.

The townsfolk worked, patching up their abodes to the best of their abilities, but they woefully lacked in supplies—much like the last state Jayden had visited. What had happened to these free states of the east? How could so much of it have been laid to waste since he'd been here the last time?

He knew the answer. The demon. He would have to fight this vile creature sooner rather than later. His stomach twisted at the thought.

Even though the Lord had provided victory for them so far, they hadn't faced a full demonic creature, only those who siphoned off the devil's power. Would this be different? Demons were said to be fallen angels, celestial beings who granted the power of the Lord, corrupted for their own means.

How could mere men compete against such things?

The others hadn't come out of their rooms yet—the innkeeper

having been generous enough to give them all individual lodging for the night. He'd said, "Not like many other visitors are going to come in through here. Might as well set you up right for your beautiful harp playing."

Jayden appreciated the compliment and the alone time.

With his friends still sleeping, getting much-needed rest after their arduous travels, and the sun just up, Jayden took a walk through the town.

He made his way toward The Demon's Eye Lake. Driftwood and debris lined the shore. The dock looked as much in disarray as the rest of the town: planks of wood missing and broken. Tradesmen hammered in new planks, replacing them.

A fisherman stood on the shore, arms crossed. He smelled of chewing tobacco, and spit some out of the side of his mouth.

"What happened here?" Jayden asked.

"Big storm," the fisherman said, not bothering to look at him, keeping his eyes on the dock. "Brought up waves from the lake like it was an ocean. They crashed down heavy on the town. Hurt many people. I don't know what's going on in these times."

"Best pray for the people," Jayden said.

"I'm not much religious."

The two men stood watching the reconstruction for a long time. Jayden wanted to help, but he'd never been handy with a hammer. Swords and instruments were the best his hands could do, and he couldn't see how his skills would be useful here.

"You're an outsider, then?" the fisherman asked after a while.

Jayden nodded. "From Hyrum."

"That's a long way."

"It is."

The fisherman finally turned to look at him. "We don't get many people out here from the west. They get uncomfortable that the Free-lands don't have lords or ladies ruling over us, but we get along just fine."

Jayden shrugged. "Some of your states are changing their ways lately, but it's not my place to criticize how you live." Or anyone, for that matter. He'd committed too many horrors when he went to war on the behalf of the Sorcerer King.

"You're a strange one, outsider."

"I am who I am."

The wind picked up along the lake, blowing gently and sounding a chime which hung off of a nearby building.

Screaming resounded in the distance.

It came from the lake, echoing all around the area. Jayden wanted to help, but couldn't think of what to do. Should he swim out into the lake? He couldn't see anything out there, as a slight haze covered the distance in the early morning sun.

"Do you have a boat?" Jayden asked.

"I do," the fisherman said.

"We should help whoever's out there," Jayden said.

"There's nothing to do. This has been the fourth disappearance in as many days. There's a reason I'm shore bound now, instead of trying to catch fish," the fisherman said.

"We have to try to help."

"You'll die if you go out there."

Jayden grimaced. "What's out in the lake?"

The fisherman stepped toward the shore. "No one knows. There is screaming and cries, and then people disappear. We haven't seen anything, but I have heard rumors there's some sort of sea monster in the lake. Many of us won't go out any longer. It's too dangerous. I don't want to lose my life for a few fish."

Jayden considered. A sea monster? A demon? Based on all he had seen, he didn't doubt it was true, but he wondered if this had to do with the prophecy. There had to be something out there. It could be tied to the storms or, or it could be something more.

"There's only one way to find out if the legends are true," Jayden said. He turned to the fisherman. "If you will not go out, will you lend me your boat? I would like to see this for myself."

"I don't much want to get my boat destroyed, either, in some foolish errand," the fisherman said. He spit out another wad of tobacco. Then his eyes softened. "But my brother disappeared three days ago. I can see you want to help. Maybe you're a man who can do something."

The fisherman stepped toward the dock and pointed. "You see the boat in the third slip from the end on the right?" he said. He pointed to a small sailing rig with oars, the sail down. The boat looked as worn as the town, but it remained afloat, even with the disrepair of the dock.

"I see it."

"If you come back, tier her up," the fisherman said.

Jayden had sailed a couple of times before, but he couldn't call himself proficient at it. He looked back at the inn. Perhaps some of his friends had awakened and might have more experience than he had. "I'll see if I can gather some help. Thank you for offering your boat. I'll get to the bottom of these disappearances, one way or another."

* * *

THE GROUP GATHERED in the common area of the inn, sitting around a circular table. The fisherman's boat could comfortably sit three people, and if they had any hopes of rescuing a poor soul, it meant only two of them could travel. "Savrin, why don't you come with me. I'll need a second."

"You know, I'm not that fond of going out on the water, especially after the Mer-folk almost killed us last time. No offense, Floryn."

"None taken," the Mer-King said. "I can swim. I am a sea creature, after all. It'll be nice to get into water again. I'd rather be there than in the boat."

Jayden looked to Floryn. "It will be helpful to have another pair of eyes with us, thank you."

"I can ride in the boat with you," Menek offered. The monk maintained such a steady resolve in being helpful. Jayden found it to be rather honorable.

He shook his head. "No, I'd rather you stay here with Bronwyn. You're the best to be with her in case something goes wrong."

Menek nodded, his eyes displaying a keen understanding of why

Jayden would want his protection over Bronwyn. He had his holy incantations, and Bronwyn seemed to have a budding ability in similar powers. If anything, he could help her grow if Jayden failed to return. Not that he didn't trust Savrin with the princess, but Menek would make a better long-term guardian. Even if he hoped it would never come to such.

Jayden cleared hs throat and refocused his thoughts on the task at hand. "The monks told us we need to travel into The Demon's Eye to confront our true enemy. We are at the edge of the lake," he said. "Our destiny lies in front of us. If we believe this to be true."

"We do," Menek interrupted.

Jayden nodded. "Whatever is blocking our path could be our enemy, perhaps be the great demon itself. But regardless, we toned to pass whatever danger is plaguing these villagers before we can go further. Even if you are tired and don't want to help with yet another town's problems, we'll have to face this for our own reasons."

"Fine, I'll go with you," Savrin said.

Jayden grinned. "Knew you'd come through."

"I miss the military. At least we got hazard pay," Savrin grumbled. "We've just been living off of others' charity since then.

Jayden patted him on the shoulder. "Let's go."

* * *

THE TWO MEN took to the boat. A soft wind blew from the west, allowing them to put up the sail to push from the dock. Floryn followed with them for a time, but soon disappeared under the water.

The air had a freshness to it. A cool breeze kissed Jayden's skin. He could get used to the sea life. Maybe when all this was over, he and Bronwyn could retire somewhere lakeside, spend time together.

It sounded so peaceful.

But he would have to survive first.

Both he and Savrin took oars, and once they'd floated a good enough distance away from the dock, they rowed in tandem, bringing the boat to brisk speeds, sailing out over the lake.

The sky had clouds in it, culminating in the north into dark puffs —storm clouds. As they rowed, those clouds grew.

They kept rowing until the shoreline disappeared. Water surrounded them on every side, with the outline of mountains along the horizon. No one else dared traverse the waters along with them.

"I don't see any other boats," Savrin said.

Jayden pointed to the water where a broken piece of wood floated. It looked like it could have come from a boat. "Look," he said.

"What happens if we end up like them?" Savrin asked.

"We won't," Jayden said. "When did you become the cautious one?"

The question quieted Savrin, who went back to rowing, peering out toward the waves on the horizon.

Floryn reappeared in front of their boat. "Greetings. I've located the ones we're looking for. They're up ahead to the northeast. You humans move so slowly on your boats."

Jayden narrowed his eyes at the Mer-King, though he couldn't fault the man for his insult. "Lead the way."

They continued along behind Floryn's lead in until the Mer-King stopped and pointed. "There!"

Jayden turned to look.

A small speck appeared on the horizon, but as he focused his eyes, the figure of a person came into view, floating in the water.

The two men went back to rowing, increasing the speed of their oars. With the sail, they made good time toward their target. Floryn kept pace beside their boat.

The man floated on a piece of driftwood, waving when he saw them. They were so far out in the lake now, it would have been difficult to swim back to shore.

Jayden pulled the boat alongside the man, dropping the sail so they wouldn't drift past him.

When they came close, the man gripped onto the side of the boat. Jayden leaned over to pull him in.

The man had a wet beard and leathery skin, hair thinning on the top of his head. "Thank the heavens someone came out here. I thought I was going to have to kick the driftwood all the way to shore—and my legs feel like they're about to fall off." He cast a strange glance at Floryn, but said nothing about the Mer-King.

"We're happy to help you. What happened out here?" Jayden asked.

The man settled into the third seat of the boat, wringing out his shirt over the side. "You won't believe me if I tell you."

"Try us," Savrin said.

The man sighed. "There's a lake monster. It reared its multiple ugly heads out of the water and shattered my boat with its tail. I'm lucky to be alive. The thing swallowed my crewmate whole."

"We've fought such creatures in the ocean. It takes an entire army of Merfolk to fell one of them."

"Really?" Jayden shook his head. "There's been many troubles in these times, all of them strange. There's a storm coming—"

"Speaking of which," Savrin said, pointing to the north. "We should return to shore. These dark clouds are picking up quickly."

Jayden picked up his oars, readying to row. "It's going to take longer to get back. Headwind is in the opposite direction. We're going to be fighting it."

Savrin shrugged. "We could tie a rope around Floryn and have him drag us."

Floryn scoffed. "I would hardly suffer such indignancy."

Jayden ignored the banter and dragged his oars to stop their momentum. Then he rowed the opposite direction. Savrin joined him. The clouds became heavier and heavier as they pushed, the sky growing darker. They wouldn't make it back before rainfall.

Wind picked up and swirled around them. Soon they would be out in dangerous conditions.

"There aren't other boats out there, are there?" Jayden asked.

"None, save some, which went out several days before. Either the monster got them or they landed elsewhere on the lake," the man said.

While Jayden preferred to search and save everyone, anyone who was out here for that long wouldn't likely be findable on the lake. He rowed as hard as he could, his arms tiring. The shore still wasn't in sight.

Moisture settled on them from the clouds, drizzling onto Jayden's face. It wasn't a full rain yet, but the greater storm wouldn't be far behind.

A wave rose in front of them, rocking the boat as it crashed, water getting splashing inside.

"This is going to get dangerous soon," Jayden said.

"Keep pushing," Savrin said, rowing hard and gritting his teeth.

"You land-walkers need to get out of here," Floyrn said before a wave gobbled him up and he disappeared under it. Jayden couldn't spot him, but he was sure the Mer-King would be fine in the situation.

The waves became fiercer, and soon their rowing did no good. Every time they made some progress, one of the giant waves pushed them back.

"We're trapped," the fisherman said, clutching the railing of the boat.

"Settle down," Jayden said. Panicking did no good. It just made hectic situations more irritating.

Scaly skin protruded from the water. Blue, almost matching the water itself, save for a glimmer of different hues.

Jayden froze. The creature. It was here with them.

"Row harder," Jayden said.

"I'm trying," Savrin said.

The scales rose from the water, like a giant snake, the torso longer and wider than the boat they sailed in. A large tail with flippers at the end flipped from the water.

The fisherman ducked inside the boat, shaking with fear.

"The boat won't give you refuge. Get back up so we can pull you into ours!" Jayden shouted to the fisherman, though he understood the man's fear. They would be helpless if the creature spotted them. Savrin didn't seem to notice the creature from his rowing position.

"What's the matter?" Savrin asked.

"Sea monster," Jayden said. The fisherman either didn't listen or hadn't heard Jayden. He remained prone in his boat.

Savrin grimaced. "I told you it was a bad idea to come out here."

"Trust in the Lord," Jayden said.

It would be all they had. They couldn't fight this sea monster alone.

Finally, the creature reared its head.

And another.

And then a third.

Three heads towered over the water, all attached to the same body. The creature had a beak jaw, beady eyes, and giant slithering tongues which shot out into the air like whips.

Each of its heads was longer than the boat itself. It could have swallowed all of them in one gulp.

The leftmost head sprung forward at them, chomping into the water, while the rightmost lashed out at the fisherman's boat.

Savrin rowed the boat to the side to make the creature miss. The fisherman's boat cracked and was destroyed in the waves.

Floryn reared his head and leveled his trident at the creature. He stabbed at its scales, but the creature was far too big for such a small object to do much damage. It merely annoyed the beast.

Jayden rowed with him to move away from the creature. He tried to get a glance at the fisherman, but saw nothing in the waves. They'd come out here to rescue the man, but they had to save their own hides now.

Would there be any way to communicate with this creature? The name of Christ and prayer easily swayed the first strange beings them faced, but as of recent encounters, it seemed not as simple. Now they fought giant beasts rather than spiritual beings. It couldn't be coincidence. The demon's power seemed to growing, manifesting in physical beings.

The three-headed beast moved too quickly for them,. It did not seem to be impacted by the wind. Rain sprayed down now, hitting Jayden in the face, making it difficult to see.

What could he do? He could try to reason with the beast.

"Sea creature," Jayden shouted. "We are on a mission from the Lord and we require passage through your lake!"

The creature reared its heads. Whether it heard or understood Jayden, he couldn't tell, but it let out a growl, the likes of which Jayden had never heard. The sound shook the waves, making the sea part around the boat. The creature's breath blew Jayden's hair harder into his face than the wind did.

The wind and rain returned soon after the breath, waves beating at the boat, rain pounding down onto the men.

Then, the center head of the creature descended. Its jaws snapped on the mast.

The fisherman jumped out of the boat immediately as the structure gave way. The center of the boat cracked. A wave descended over their vessel as the creature's head smacked against it.

Savrin flew from the boat, yelling as the wave shot him through the air and out into the water.

Floryn, who still attacked the creature with his trident, spotted Savrin and dove after the rogue. He went underwater and disappeared along with Savrin.

Jayden remained steady, even though the creature's descent smashed the boat in half. He still floated and remained seated, despite Savrin getting pulled underwater. Even though he worried for the rogue, he didn't have time to look for him at the moment. He had to take the opportunity to counterstrike. Gaining a careful balance, he raised his oar and slammed it against the creature's skull.

The sea monster's skin proved as hard as a rock The wooden oar snapped on contact. The creature descended back into the water as if nothing happened.

Jayden gripped his bench in small corner of the boat, staying afloat for now. Once another wave hit, he would have to find some other means to stay out of the water.

Savrin was nowhere in sight still, nor was Floryn. The fisherman swam away as fast as he could. So much for allies. What could he do?

The sea monster dove beneath the waves as rain descended harder. Lightning struck in the distance, and thunder roared, the entire sky crackling in a brilliant light.

"Savrin! Floryn!" Jayden shouted, hoping to find his companions.

He received no answer.

The tail of the sea monster burst from the water, flapping and hitting the surface once more.

A wave crashed against Jayden's corner of the boat. It filled with water and sank. His boots became soaked, and Jayden sank into the water.

He treaded the water as best he could, but a wave crashed into his face, filling his throat and nostrils with water. The crash came so suddenly he couldn't stop his breathing, inhaling too much of the lake. He coughed and couldn't catch his breath.

Raising its ugly heads again, the monster roared and opened three jaws wide. The sounds traveled in multiple directions, overwhelming Jayden as he struggled to stay afloat.

The beast scanned the areasearching for its prey. Jayden kept his head low to the water as best he could, hoping he could evade the creature's notice.

Then, he spotted Savrin.

The rogue had daggers in hands and swam toward the sea monster. As he came closer, Floryn's body popped up from the waves. Savrin rode atop the Mer-King's back. The rogue raised both blades, sticking them into one of the creature's three necks. He grabbed hold of the edge of one of its scales as the sea monster flailed.

The Mer-King's trident hadn't done much damage, and Jayden presumed those dagger cuts couldn't have done much to truly bother the creature. Savrin grabbed onto the blades and the creature thrashed, flailing Savrin about in the air. His attack may not have been the best of ideas.

Another head ducked, down biting at the neck where Savrin stabbed.

Floryn intercepted the attacking head, jabbing his trident into its throat and pinning its jaw. It didn't last for long; the monster shook its head, and the trident went flying. But it had been enough of a distraction to keep the rogue from being eaten alive.

Savrin used his weight to kick off of the sea monster, getting out of its clutches and splashing back into the water.

The third head took aim for Jayden. Its jaws crashed into the water, missing him, but its forehead slamming into Jayden anyway. The blow forced Jayden deep underwater, catching Jayden mid-breath. More water filled his lungs and nostrils.

Jayden kept his eyes open. With the sky above so cloudy, he couldn't see much. The water had a black coloration to it. He hoped the sea monster couldn't see much better than he did.

Regardless, he had to get back to surface. He pushed with his legs and arms to bring himself up as quickly as he could. His lungs burned, starved for breath, but he was discombobulated, unable to figure out which way to swim.

Thankfully, a pair of arms grabbed him and pulled him to the surface. Floryn tread water next to him as they breached through to the surface.

The sea monster still lived, however, honing in on Savrin, who swam away as quickly as he could. The fisherman floated off to the left—face down, his limp body carried by the waves. They'd failed in saving him.

Jayden coughed and caught his breath, then muttered a prayer for the soul of the fisherman.

Perhaps it had been hubris to travel out into the lake like this alone with Savrin. They'd handled all of their problems so far—by the grace of God, but there had been warnings of the lake being much worse than anything they'd faced so far.

He understood now why the lake was named The Demon's Eye.

But what could he do now? They had no way to get back to shore. This monster would hunt them down.

*Lord, please deliver us from this evil.*

The sea monster head-butted Savrin much in the manner it had done to Jayden. The rogue fell to the side, waves rising and crashing around him. Rain poured down.

A light came from behind him, shining on everything.

Jayden turned, the light too bright for him to see much. But there was a boat, and a figure of a man standing at its bow. Jayden shaded his eyes to get a better look.

* * *

BEHIND THE LIGHT, Menek stood in a boat. The light floated in the air, and Menek maintained prayers to keep the divine power flowing. Bronwyn sat in the boat with him.

Floryn swam off further, grabbing hold of Savrin, with one arm, and holding his recovered trident in the other. He pushed Savrin up over the side of Menek's boat to keep him from drowning. Savrin looked like he'd inhaled too much water, coughing and choking—but he was alive.

"Go back! It's too dangerous!" Jayden shouted.

He should have been glad to see them. They might be the only way he could come out of this alive, but he'd rather they survive, if it were up to him.

The three-headed sea monster roared, snapping its jaws and jerking its head around. The motion caused waves to form around it, lifting Jayden up and dragging him back down as it receded.

He treaded water as best he could.

Menek kept chanting, the light still shining above him. Whatever power the monk channeled, it was great and holy.

The sea monster recoiled from it as they came closer. Its center head let out a loud bellow, which echoed across the lake.

Then it charged the boat.

Floryn held his trident out of the water, aiming it toward the sea monster's middle head. He shouted something in his Mer language.

The sea monster froze when it heard the Mer-King speak. It made a strange sound from its middle head. Jayden spoke to it earlier, but he hadn't thought of having Floryn try. Perhaps it had simply not understood the language.

Floryn continued talking to it.

Jayden swam toward the boat. Menek and Bronwyn pulled him up into it.

"I'm glad you're safe," Bronwyn said.

"I told you it was a bad idea to come out here," Savrin said.

"We're even now," Jayden said. "For all the bad plans you've had."

He'd been right, but Jayden had to try. He wasn't interested in arguing semantics with Savrin right now. He peered over the boat to watch the interaction between Floryn and the sea monster.

The two communicated as the storm raged on. Menek's boat rocked and swayed. Lightning flashed in the sky. Floryn and the sea monster continued to speak with each other in the foreign language.

Eventually, the sea monster lowered its head. Floryn crawled onto it, turning to face the boat. He waved.

"The creature is going to help us! Its name is Gr'wrr!" Floryn said.

Jayden laughed at the ridiculousness of the situation. He'd nearly died a few moments prior, and now Floyn rode the creature as if it were a mount.

"You couldn't have talked to it sooner?" Jayden asked.

The Mer-King shrugged. "I couldn't know the creature would speak Mer. We are a long way from the ocean. I wished it an honorable death, and it understood me to be more than a mere beast or demon. A delightful creature."

"Not the word I'd use, but I'm glad it's on our side," Jayden said.

"What now?" Menek asked. As his chant ended, the light faded, and the monk looked to Jayden for guidance.

"We should head back and regroup. This storm isn't natural any more than the sea monster is," Jayden said. "I'd like to know what Floryn said to the creature to tame it."

"Me as well," Menek said.

The monk turned the boat around and rowed them back. Floryn followed on the head of the sea monster.

# INTERLUDE

Interlude Three

When they returned to the inn, Jayden took some time for a much needed bath. The warm water soaked through to his bones, making him tired enough to fall asleep in the tub before the innkeeper came to retrieve him.

The others gathered around the table, frothy mugs of beer poured before all but Bronwyn, who drank tea. Jayden paused to grasp the context of their conversation.

"Gr'wrr told me violent shaking under the sea awakened him and then agitated him. He didn't know who was responsible and so lashed out, but it seems he is thousands of years old and has been sleeping for a long time. The creature doesn't understand what years are, which perplexed him, but he was to look for the sign of the Mer in the lake to complete his cause," Floryn said.

"I suppose there haven't been Mer in this lake for a long time, if ever," Savrin said.

"The ancients who gave him the descriptions understood well enough. Though I wonder how they received such a prophecy," Floryn said.

"The Lord works in mysterious ways," Menek said. His eyes flicked over to Jayden. "Speaking of prophecy…"

Being some sort of chosen arbiter of prophecy still made Jayden uneasy. He shifted his weight to one leg out of habit. "Hello," he said, joining the others at the table.

"Look who's finally back among the living," Savrin said, raising his glass to Jayden. "Want one?"

"I'll abstain for now."

"Of course you will," Savrin said, gulping down the last of the liquid in his mug.

"Continue," Jayden said, motioning to Floryn. "I've been meaning to ask you how you swayed the sea monster."

Floryn nodded. "There isn't much story to tell. He recognized my visage and understood my language. Gr'wrr is quite reasonable. He told me the ancients gave him commands to serve me and my companions as is the will of the one true God. Simple enough."

It sounded simple enough, but also too good to be true.

Jayden took an empty chair and crossed his arms. "And you trust this creature?"

"One thing about creatures of the sea—or anywhere—they are not like men. They have their instincts, they have their solid purposes. They do not lie or fight amongst themselves. The concept is foreign to them, as they have no souls or ability for discernment."

"Man might say that about the Mer," Savrin said.

Floryn glowered at him. "Careful. Your jokes come dangerously close to insults, which require retribution."

Savrin held his hands up. "Hey, I can't land all of my lines."

From Jayden's experience, the Mer-King spoke truth. Creatures acted as to their natures. Rarely would one be capable of stealth or deception.

"He's going to help us," Jayden said.

"Yes," Floryn said. "Though his domain is the lake. He can't leave it."

"And if the ancients led us to this creature, it must be part of our purposeful path," Menek said.

Jayden stroked his chin. "I'm inclined to agree."

All eyes turned to him. Despite not wanting the responsibility, they looked to him as a leader. He would have to act as one if they were to move forward.

"Everything's been leading us to this juncture," Jayden said. "The ancients have been so purposeful in their path that I can't believe they arbitrarily named The Demon's Eye. With the sea monster sent to serve us, I have to believe our trials and path have prepared us to reach this point."

Menek's eyes twinkled, seeming to approve of his words. The monk had tremendous faith. Jayden wished his own could be as strong.

"Our next task will be the culmination of everything we've experienced," Jayden said. "We're meant to draw on our understandings of magicks, spirits, and infernal creations. Our trials had purpose. And it means we also have not faced the worst of what's to come."

"I never should have gone treasure hunting," Savrin said.

"Probably not." Jayden grinned.

"But here we are," Bronwyn said, her eyes locking with Jayden's. "For better or for worse."

The words sent chills through Jayden's spine, words he hoped to say to her in return once they came safely away from all of this. When he could provide and care for her for the rest of their days.

When he'd set out on this adventure, he'd had little purpose in this life. Leaving the Sorcerer King's employ and trying to avoid the horrors of war made him wander. Music had been a part of the wandering, but it also was the one thing that brought him solace.

Performing brought him a sense of aliveness which no other activity could. The moments of music felt so pure—much like the sight of Bronwyn's eyes.

Those moments also proved fleeting.

By contrast, a divine purpose like this prophecy, facing evil, and ensuring the salvation of everyone in the world, provided true joy. When it was over, he had a different long-term purpose with Bronwyn. This was the life he'd been predestined to have.

It brought Jayden new confidence, and his friends shared confidence in him. He wouldn't let them down.

"I believe we're meant to go to the heart of this storm, the center of The Demon's Eye. The evil we seek emanates from there, and we have the strength to deal with it. The Lord provides for us."

Long faces surrounded the table. The party had been through too much death and destruction as of late. These people needed morale.

"We've faced down the Sorcerer King, overcome pits of doom, giant beasts, wraiths," Jayden said. He slammed his fist on the table. "Now we're going to the source of all these troubles." He leaned in. "We will not fail."

"Yeah!" Savrin shouted, clenching his fist.

"We can do anything through He who strengthens us," Menek said.

Floryn inclined his head. "I am proud to be a part of this team."

Bronwyn smiled.

Live or die—they would do it together, in communion. It was the way the world was meant to be.

"We rest for a day and then we head out. We will ride Gr'wrr into battle," Jayden said. "Relax and have fun for now. This may be the last chance we get."

Savrin motioned to the innkeeper. "Another round, please!"

## 12

THE PARTY RODE ON THE THREE NECKS OF THE GIANT SEA MONSTER, which allowed them to strap leather saddles around it as if it were a horse. Menek and Savrin had their own heads to ride, while Bronwyn wrapped her arms tightly around Jayden.

It felt good having her there. As she breathed, her breasts pushed against his back. He tried his best not to think about the sensation while scanning the waters for Floryn, who took to the lake along with the creature.

The sky blackened as they approached the center of the storm, the middle of The Demon's Eye, where maps showed there should have been a small series of islands. They could not see any land in the raining dark.

Lightning flashed, illuminating everything around them. Still no sign of land.

Had this storm had swallowed the islands?

Anything was possible. After the adventures he'd had, Jayden wouldn't have blinked to have been told the islands themselves were parts of the demon they would face.

He hoped they could contain it.

His harp remained secure on the sea monster's neck, ready for him to play the song of the ancients.

Would that be all it took? It seemed all too easy. Perhaps it would require more of them to bind this demon again. Time would tell. The Lord would show the way.

Ahead of them, a pulsing funnel of pure darkness loomed within the storm. The sea monster almost swam into it, but stopped when Floryn commanded it to halt.

Jayden couldn't get a clear view of the funnel. The darkness blended into everything else from a distance. But when he focused, it stood out in the storm.

The dark swirled like a portal in front of them. Would this be some entrance into the spirit realm?

Being near it made Jayden's hair stand on his arms. A natural instinct to run away from this place swept over him. It was pure evil.

"Do we have to go in there?" Bronwyn asked.

Jayden peered at the swirling black. He couldn't say for certain, but he sensed it was the place they would have to go. This would be where they'd make their stand against this demon.

"It's our calling," Jayden said.

"I had a bad feeling you were going to say that," Savrin said.

Jayden undid his straps, then carefully slid around the side of the sea monster's head to loosen his harp. Once he had it secured on his back, he climbed atop the sea monster's skull, offering a hand to Bronwyn to help her up.

She joined him. "What do you think's on the other side?"

Jayden frowned. "Hell. Or a close approximation of it."

Fear crossed Bronwyn's eyes. She squeezed Jayden's arm.

"Don't be afraid. This is what I was destined to do. What happens here is part of God's plan."

"It will take strong faith to get through this," Menek said.

Floryn swam ahead, close to the edge of the darkness. "Say the word," he said.

Jayden took Bronwyn's hand. "We go together," he said.

Bronwyn nodded.

They jumped off the head of the sea monster toward the darkness. When they crossed the threshold into the darkness, Jayden tensed from the deep cold.

Then, they fell.

* * *

HELL WOULD HAVE BEEN an apt description for what Jayden experienced, or at least purgatory.

Blackness surrounded him. Worse than any night or storm he'd ever encountered. A complete absence of light. He lost hold of Bronwyn's hand somewhere along the descent, detaching him from his only warmth, the only semblance of light in the world.

The cold pierced all around him, his clothes not providing a shield against the blackness. Being wet from the storm didn't help, but at least they hadn't soaked themselves in the sea. He could only imagine what Floryn must have felt in here, though the Mer-King had a body much more attuned to colder climates.

The falling sensation disoriented him. Within the blackness, Jayden couldn't tell which way was up or down. No wind struck at his back to give him a clearer sensation. His stomach churned.

"Bronwyn?" Jayden asked in a gasp. He couldn't see her, and all he wanted was to know she was safe.

If she screamed or called out for him, he couldn't hear her.

The ground hit with a shocking suddenness, ramming into his shoulder first.

Jayden's teeth chattered. The harp case clanged against him, making discordant sounds and also pressing weight against his back. Jayden winced.

As much as Jayden wanted to lie there and recover from the hellish experience of the descent through darkness, they had to keep moving. Every moment they wasted brought them closer to this demon wreaking havoc upon their world.

Jayden pushed himself to his feet, dusting off the dirt. "Is everyone here?"

"Yes, but I jammed my wrist something fierce," Savrin said.

"I've made it," Menek said.

"Likewise," Floryn said.

Bronwyn didn't answer.

Jayden still couldn't see where Bronwyn had landed, and without her voice responding, it caused him to stiffen with nerves. "Bronwyn?" he asked again.

"Oh, sorry," Bronwyn said. "We jumped together. I assumed you knew I was down here."

Savrin chuckled. "It's the apocalypse and they're flirting. How cute."

Jayden scanned the area, but it was too dark to make anything out. "Menek, can you do your prayer to make light?"

"On it," Menek said. He began chanting in an ancient language.

Soon, a glow appeared from over his head, illuminating their surroundings.

They stood on a bed of sandy dirt, soft, even though it hadn't felt like it when they hit the ground. Rock walls rose all around them. A large pit. There didn't appear to be any entrances or exits.

Jayden frowned. This wasn't what he'd expected when he'd entered the darkness. It seemed such an anti-climactic, still place. No wind blew here. The air was dead and stale.

What had he expected? In the back of his mind he'd thought of an ancient temple, ornate carvings, a dais. Wouldn't demons want followers and sacrifices?

Something shrieked above them. It dawned on Jayden that the dragon or demon or whatever it was had lured them here. They were trapped in a pit for the creature to swoop down upon.

"Are we going to deal with another giant snake?" Savrin asked.

In answer to Savrin's question, a loud roar came from above.

"I don't think that's a snake," Floryn said.

"It's likely the demon. Brace yourselves," Jayden said.

Swooping down from the darkness came a giant creature—red, scaly, the direct opposite of the water monster they'd seen. It had long-spanning wings like a giant bat, but a long neck and face of a snake. Its tongue slithered into the air in front of it, as if testing the winds, and then it belched deep flames, covering the cavern in fire.

Jayden covered Bronwyn, holding her down. Immense heat covered Jayden's back. It was hot, but it didn't feel like he'd been burned.

"Dragon!" Savrin shouted.

Floryn readied his trident and chucked it.

The trident flew toward the creature but clanked into its red scales, dropping to the earth for Floryn to scurry and recover.

The dragon seemed to understand Floryn's intent, turning in its flight to swerve toward the Mer-King.

Menek changed his chant. His light expanded from him, creating a golden shimmer in front of a cowering Floryn.

The dragon flew into the shimmering light-shield. The creature recoiled, screeching. It then sprayed the area in flame again.

"I'll be fine," Bronwyn whispered from beneath Jayden, pushing him lightly. She seemed to have more than staying protected on her mind, as a soft glow formed around her. Magick radiated in the air.

Jayden got to his feet, surveying the situation. They wouldn't last long against this creature—be it the demon or simply one of its guardians.

He scrambled backward, trying to find a safe space near one wall to get his harp out. He wasn't sure it was time to play his song, but he had to try.

The harp caught in its case. Jayden did his best to tug it free.

The dragon turned its eye to him, swooping to the ground, landing in a puff of dust. It trudged forward on four limbs, leaving clawed track marks in the dirt.

Menek chanted more, a similar shield of energy appearing in front of Jayden as the one that had Floryn. The dragon spotted it, briefly pausing in his advance.

Jayden got the harp out of the case. He plucked a chord.

The dragon howled, but the sound did little other than annoy the creature. It pushed forward, head-butting into Menek's shield.

The light flickered. Menek tensed. The monk chanted louder.

The dragon head-butted again.

This time, the shield failed.

Stumbling forward, the dragon crashed the top of its skull into the harp. It made a discordant sound which echoed in the cavern.

Jayden couldn't keep hold of the instrument as he tumbled into the rocky sidewall. The edges of the rock face cut through Jayden's clothing.

Bronwyn moved for the harp to grab it, her magic flowing into the instrument and causing it to glow along with her. She infused the ancient's instrument with new power.

The dragon reared its head again, growling and opening its maw to bite Jayden's head off.

Before it could, Savrin swept in, stabbing the creature in the neck with his daggers.

Much like Savrin had done with the sea monster, he cut between the scales, in a tender spot where his knives could get hold. He pulled, tearing dragon flesh.

The creature bucked its head back.

The force carried Savrin into the air, who kept his grip on the dragon by clutching his knives trapped in its neck. "Whoa!" Savrin shouted.

Bronwyn rushed to Jayden's side, harp in her hand. "Here," she said.

The events dazed Jayden so much he'd almost forgotten to act. It was good he had the princess by his side. He smiled at her. "Thank you."

"Don't mention it. Play your heart out," she said, eyes twinkling.

Floryn tried to get to a position to hit the dragon with his trident. Most of his blows clanked against the dragon's scales, but once or twice he connected with flesh. Savrin's daggers penetrated at the same time as one of Floryn's strikes. The dragon howled in pain. It blasted fire onto the walls.

Rocks fell from the cave walls, hitting the dirt below with a sizzle, heated by the dragon's breath.

Jayden exhaled slowly. He had to concentrate. The world around him didn't matter, only the song.

He plucked the opening notes of the song of the ancients, letting the melody flow through him, focusing on accuracy. With the help of Bronwyn's magick, the notes seemed to do more than merely project sound this time. The sounds had an energy which Jayden could feel through all of his senses. Warmth invaded his touch. Brightness filled his eyes. The scent of roses filled his nostrils. And a taste like the finest wine crossed his tongue.

The others kept the dragon occupied while he played, Savrin stabbing with one arm after another, flailing through the air but keeping his grip on the dagger hilts to stay atop the dragon. The rogue got himself up onto the dragon's neck, gripping at the top of one of its scales.

"Woo! I got my own mount!"

The dragon tried to buck him off, flapping its wings and taking to the air again.

Jayden continued his playing. The song flowed through his fingers, vibrating to his very soul as he plucked strings.

Floryn changed tactics to target the dragon's wings. His trident punctured a hole through the thin membrane. The creature was not as impervious as it had appeared at first.

But the song did nothing, even with the help of Bronwyn's magick. The dragon didn't seem to take any note of it whatsoever. What had gone wrong?

Jayden played the song perfectly, he was sure of it. He'd practiced the song at length so many times, he could perform it in his sleep.

"It's not working," Bronwyn said.

"No, it's not," Jayden said.

Menek prayed. He then opened his eyes and breathed out at the dragon—flame much like from a dragon itself.

The dragon flailed, rearing its head up, but the flames didn't harm the creature.

Jayden set the harp aside and reached for his sword. Did they need to fight this creature? Was this the wrong time to be playing the song?

Throughout this journey, Jayden wanted to avoid violence in favor of something like music, or finding a thoughtful way to resolve situations, but he kept being brought back to the sword. It was as if his former life followed him, creeping up behind him and invading his space.

He let the hilt of his sword go. No, he had to remain pure if he were to perform the task the Lord set before him. Much as he had to keep Bronwyn at a distance to maintain the purity of his body, keeping his sword sheathed would maintain the purity of his soul.

But the song didn't work. All he could do was watch.

*Let go...*

It was like a voice came directly into his skull, but Jayden couldn't see anyone speaking to him. Menek raised his voice in his chanting, Bronwyn stood in the shadows, while Savrin and the Mer-King did the fighting. Where had the voice come from?

What did it mean?

He considered, watching Savrin dice the dragon's neck.

Over the course of these events of the last several weeks, Jayden needed to control everything. He directed their paths, came up with the solutions.

Was this what the voice meant? To let go? To trust his friends.

This was the team he'd assembled, his friends, his family. The people who mattered.

Yes, this task wouldn't be up to him—he had to trust the others as he trusted in God.

This was his test.

Jayden moved back into a protective stance in front of Bronwyn. Her life meant more than his in the scheme of things. When they completed their task here, she would have a kingdom to preside over.

"What are you doing?" Bronwyn asked.

"Letting my friends handle this," Jayden said.

Floryn continued to shred the dragon's left wing with his trident, slithering around to the other side of the creature to do the same to its other wing. Red blood splattered all over the cavern floor.

Fire erupted from its mouth, lighting up the darkness above.

The fire died in the blackness.

And then the dragon died.

It fell from the sky with one last desperate howl.

Savrin fell with it, crashing down again, landing atop the creature.

"Savrin!" Bronwyn shouted, rushing forward. "Are you all right?"

The rogue lay still, but then slid off the dragon's neck, taking the daggers with him.

"Savrin—dragon slayer! That has quite the ring to it." Savrin grinned. He pointed to Jayden. "You'd best write an epic song about this to be sung through the ages."

Jayden chuckled. "I will."

Quiet fell over the cavern, even Menek stopping his chants.

Was this it? Nothing seemed to change. No portal appeared. No way out. Nor did any other danger present itself.

"Are we done?" Bronwyn asked.

"I don't know," Jayden said, frowning. He peered at the dragon carcass. An enormous creature, but just flesh in the end. It didn't seem so frightening now.

Then, the dragon's eyes shot open.

* * *

THE EYES WERE BEADIER than before, like a great evil inhabited them.

The dragon's flesh melted away, revealing bloody meat like a slaughtered animal. Then, even that peeled back to its bones.

The others grabbed their weapons, stepping back and away from the creature. This wouldn't be the end after all.

Once the flesh evaporated, a smoky darkness remained. But the dragon's eyes remained in the shadowy form. Those eyes stayed locked on Jayden.

A tendril of the smoke reached out, wrapping around Jayden. It lifted him into the air.

He tried to squirm out of the tendril's grasp, but nothing worked.

Menek resumed his chanting, bringing light forth. The darkness recoiled from it and dropped Jayden to the ground.

Jayden inhaled sharply as he hit the dirt, his lower back in pain from too much jolting and from where he'd scraped against the rocks before.

When he did, the darkness entered him.

It was cold, much like the portal above, but a different cold. This one permeated throughout him, impossible to escape from.

He tried to scream, but no sound came from his lips.

Then the world faded.

* * *

Jayden stood in a room made of metal. It reminded him of the strange chambers of the ancients he and Savrin had first discovered when they traveled the mountains of the Freelands.

A man appeared across from him, wearing all red, a strange type of attire with a long piece of cloth dangling from his neck to about his navel. His black hair was slicked back and looked like it was wet—but it held in place. What was most striking was he had the same yellow eyes as the dragon.

"You're the demon," Jayden said, instinctively reaching for his sword. It wasn't at his hip.

"And this is my domain. Do you think I'd let you have a weapon? Not as if one could hurt me, I suppose," the demon said, pacing around Jayden. "Still, it would do no good to have you stabbing me."

"Why have you brought me here?" Jayden asked, eyes locked on the strange man.

"We've discussed this before. Don't you remember your dream?"

Jayden recalled the strange dream he'd had along the journey. The demon had tempted him through a dream, asking Jayden to join him and rule the world. It seemed so long ago, though Jayden had shown enough resolve that the demon had not returned.

"I'm just a soul like you," the demon said, motioning over his body. "Whether in this form or another. Would you prefer a woman? Would that soften your heart?'

The demon's visage shimmered out, and then the creature reappeared as Bronwyn.

Jayden stumbled backward. "Father of lies."

The image of Bronwyn giggled. "Not quite." Her lush lips protruded as she pouted. "What's the matter? Don't you like me?"

"I've been chaste with the real Bronwyn. There's no way a vile Jezebel will sway me," Jayden said.

The fake Bronwyn clicked her tongue. "Too bad. We could have so much fun together. But regardless, we can still discuss what's to come."

"I will not make a deal with you, nor will I succumb to any temptations of the flesh," Jayden said.

"You sound so calculating. How about this?" The false Bronwyn leaned in close. "Your friends are all going to die by asphyxiation, or you can stop this fight now. Your choice."

Jayden froze, trying not to show any fear or sign of weakness. The demon wanted him to react. It was the whole point. He would remain strong.

"I can see in your eyes this worries you. It's good, healthy to be concerned for your friends. Tell me, do you know much about me?"

"Only that you are evil," Jayden said.

"The ancients picked me up by mistake on their way here. I inhabited and possessed a few of them, killed many more. It took them a long time to figure out it wasn't merely their cook who slaughtered so many of them." False Bronwyn grinned. "I fled when they reached this world and set down humanity's footprint on what was once a rock. Did you know they had the hubris of God, thinking they could create their own world?"

Jayden said nothing.

False Bronwyn circled him. "No matter. The hundreds of people lost their lives trying to capture me. What chance do you think you have?"

Jayden had enough. This creature had played on his baser instincts —lust, fear, anger. He wouldn't let it get the best of him. "Let me out of here. I stand in the glory of the Lord Jesus Christ by whom all things are made. By his name, release me!"

The demon wailed, shriveling from the form of Bronwyn into a dark mist with deadly yellow eyes. It couldn't maintain its shape.

Jayden stepped toward it. "The Lord Jesus Christ protects me!"

The words caused the demon to shriek again. This time, reality broke around Jayden. It shattered like glass in front of his eyes; the room giving way.

* * *

HE CAME to consciousness again in the cavern, his friends gathered around him. Bronwyn—the real one—had her hand on his face.

The smoky darkness permitted all around them and then coalesced on Bronwyn's head.

"Get back!" Jayden said.

The warning came too late. The demon filled her. She convulsed, and her eyes spun into the back of her head. Then Bronwyn levitated.

"I see why you like this body so much," the demon said, its voice coming out of Bronwyn like the sound of a cat scratching on wood.

"Let go of her," Jayden shouted, scrambling to his feet.

Floryn pointed his trident toward Bronwyn.

"Now, now, you're not going to shoot my new form. You were so rude to my last one." Fire blasted from Bronwyn's eyes, knocking the trident from Floryn's hand and setting it ablaze. The weapon hit the ground, fire crackling.

Floryn scooted backward, dumbfounded.

Jayden used the moment of distraction to move to his harp. The demon lost its focus on him and gave him moments to get set and play the song of the ancients.

Bronwyn rushed him, but Savrin dove in front of him, tackling Bronwyn to the ground.

Jayden's fingers floated across the harp strings.

The demon flung Savrin across the cavern. The rogue rolled in the dirt. He didn't get up. Snarling with Bronwyn's mouth, the demon moved forward.

This time, Menek brought up a prayer shield in front of Jayden to allow him to keep playing the song unmolested.

Jayden didn't rush the tune. Changing the tempo might cause problems with whatever this song was supposed to do. As much as he wanted to hurry through it, he kept his fingers steadily plucking the notes in time. It sounded right.

The demon slammed Bronwyn's fists against the shield over and over. They bloodied. Then the creature smashed Bronwyn's head into the shield.

"You have to stop it. The evil is going to kill Bronwyn!" Floryn shouted.

It was all meant to distract Jayden, to make it so he couldn't play. He had to stay strong, resolved. The demon tested him, but he wouldn't succumb. The harp sounded through the cavern—he was nearly halfway through the song.

When Bronwyn slammed her head against the shield again, Menek caved. He dropped the shield, stopping his chanting. The demon to advance on Jayden again.

The monk wouldn't allow Bronwyn through, however. He tackled her, much as Savrin had before, sending her tumbling to the ground.

Jayden kept his fingers moving on the harp strings, hoping he would have enough time. He wanted to chastise Menek, but it would do no good. The monk did as he felt was right.

Bronwyn flung Menek away with uncanny strength, and soon there was nothing but the harp between Bronwyn and Jayden.

Only a few more bars, and the song would be complete. He plucked the strings.

The demon struggled. It seemed to have difficulty controlling Bronwyn. She lashed out with her own hands against herself. Her nails scratched down her face, causing her to bleed.

It was a horrific sight. Jayden could hardly keep himself from putting a stop to it. But the demon wanted him to stop. He had to finish his mission. God had brought him here to use his gift of playing.

Bronwyn's head spun around on her neck several times, as if it had become detached. The demon screamed as the final notes of the song played.

Jayden finished the song, exhaling. He'd given the best performance he could muster. True glory to God.

The demon spewed out of Bronwyn's mouth as if she had vomited it out. Then she collapsed to the ground. Her head appeared normal, as if the demon had never been inside her, but the bloody knuckles and her wounded face were a reminder of what had controlled her these last minutes.

The mist had trouble forming, even its eyes shaking and convulsing. Then it burst, darkness shattering across the pit.

The images around them also changed, the walls falling, the darkness dissipating. The ground beneath them shook, cracking open in the center of the pit.

There, the darkness of the demon funneled into the crack. It whirled, wind picking up, knocking Jayden's harp from his hands. It was all he could do to keep himself standing.

The others around him all lay unconscious on the ground, save for Floryn, who struggled along with him.

Once the demon was in the ground, the pit quaked again, sealing it inside. The winds stopped. The blackness above disappeared, revealing a blue sky. The clouds parted, a rainbow forming above them, bright and more beautiful than Jayden had ever seen.

Jayden's eyes regained focus around them, and he could see they stood on an island. The center of The Demon's Eye, as they had intended.

The storm receded, bringing calm to the giant lake.

The downed men stirred, so Jayden moved to Bronwyn, dropping to his knees beside her. Blood dripped off of her, though the wounds had already started to heal. Her hair was matted and dirty, but she still breathed. He held her in his arms until she awoke.

"My eyes," Bronwyn said.

"We'll ensure you receive the best healers possible," Jayden said.

"Did we win?" she asked.

"Yes." Jayden never had a doubt.

Bronwyn smiled, then lost consciousness again.

# EPILOGUE

"I now pronounce you husband and wife," Menek said, raising his arms and then stepping back.

Bronwyn pushed toward Jayden. He wrapped his arms around her. They kissed.

Jayden dipped Bronwyn for the crowd's reaction. The people hooted and hollered. Even mid-kiss, he couldn't help but break into a smile.

"It's amazing to think two weeks ago we were facing down an actual demon," Bronwyn said. Since then, Menek and the monks had worked their healing to remove any of the deep gashes and resulting scars from the demon. She looked as beautiful as ever.

"I don't want to think about it now," Jayden said. The trial was over. They'd won. More importantly, for his immediate future, his need to maintain celibacy ended along with it.

They jogged down the aisle way together, a red carpet in the middle of St. Timothy's Cathedral, Hyrum's largest church, and now a makeshift headquarters for the Church Vigilant. Ordinarily, the bishop would have performed any ceremony here, but the church made a special exception for Menek, given their close bond with the monk.

Gatherers threw rice, a tradition thousands of years old, one in which Jayden couldn't understand the significance. Bronwyn hurried through the crowd to a carriage—driven by Jayden's best man, Savrin. They hopped in and closed the door behind them.

Cheers continued outside. The people of Hyrum loved their princess and could hardly contain their glee for her wedding. No one wanted to remember the tyrannical reign of the Sorcerer King. This wedding would make for a clean break and a fresh start

The whole world had become a better place because of their quest. His body seemed to float on air. Jayden leaned his head back against a cushion in the carriage. He could finally relax.

"It surprised me," Bronwyn said.

"Hmm?" Jayden asked.

"Asking me to marry you," Bronwyn said. "I knew you had affection for me, but you kept being so distant. I thought you might enter the priesthood."

Jayden snorted. "It's not for me. I like..." he let his eyes drift over her supple body, only further refined by the tight corset beneath her wedding dress. "...the finer things."

Bronwyn laughed softly. Her eyes shone at him. "You're supposed to court a woman at least a while."

Jayden shrugged. "I know what I want."

She smiled. "Me too."

They leaned into one another, kissing each other once more. While the public declaration of their love had been one thing, in private, Jayden could fully savor the sweet taste of her lips. He didn't want to break the moment, but a bump in the road forced them apart.

"Perhaps we should wait until we get back to the palace," Bronwyn said.

"Good idea."

They sat in silence for a time, before Bronwyn reached over and took his hand. "Taking the throne will be a daunting task. I prepared for it all of my life, but I never imagined it actually happening."

Jayden shifted, but he held her hand. He kept his mouth shut, not knowing what to say.

The palace appeared ahead of them, the sun setting in the background and shining on the stone walls, washing everything with a reddish color. Beautiful, nearly as much so as his new bride. This was the perfect scene. And by the Lord, he couldn't wait to get to their chamber and consummate the marriage.

"Have you given much thought to being king?" Bronwyn asked.

Jayden nearly choked. He forgot to breathe for several long moments. No, he hadn't thought about kingship. It had never occurred to him, despite the proposal and marriage, that he would become a monarch.

Suddenly, he wondered if he'd made a mistake, not for himself with Bronwyn, but for the people of Hyrum. King Jayden. Oh, Lord.

"You're turning pale," Bronwyn said. "Oh, my. You'd forgotten you married a princess, hadn't you?'

"I didn't think it through," Jayden said.

Bronwyn laughed. "Want to annul?"

"Not on your life," Jayden said, planting another kiss on her lips for good measure.

Like so many matters these last several months, marriage came as a new adventure. One he would share with a beautiful woman beside him.

# ALSO BY JON DEL ARROZ

**The Adventures Of Baron Von Monocle:**

*For Steam And Country*

*The Blood Of Giants*

*The Fight For Rislandia*

*The Iron Wedding*

The Steam Knight

The Crystal Conspiracy

**The Nano Templar Series**

*Justified*

*Sanctified*

*Glorified*

**The Aryshan War**

*The Stars Entwined*

*The Stars Asunder*

*The Stars Rejoined*

*Colony Launch*